EMLYN'S MOON

THE MAGICIAN TRILOGY

BOOK TWO

JENNY NIMMO

ORCHARD BOOKS

AN IMPRINT OF SCHOLASTIC INC.

NEW YORK

For my mother

LIBRARY OF CONGRESS CATALOGING-IN-PUBLICATION DATA

Nimmo, Jenny.
Emlyn's Moon / Jenny Nimmo. — 1st ed.
p. cm. — (The magician trilogy; bk. 2)
First published: Great Britain: Methuen Children's Books Ltd., 1986. 1st American edition published under the title, Orchard of the Cresent Moon: New York: Dutton, 1989.
Sequel to The Snow Spider.
Summary: Nia, the middle girl in a large Welsh family, discovers her own special artistic talent as she uncovers the dark secret shared by the Llewelyn and Griffiths families.
ISBN 13: 978-0-439-84676-9
ISBN 10: 0-439-84676-5
[1. Magic — Fiction. 2. Wales — Fiction.] I. Title.
II. Series: Nimmo, Jenny. Magician Trilogy; bk. 2.
PZ7.N5897Eml 2007
[Fic] — dc22   2006009855
10 9 8 7 6 5 4 3 2 1   07 08 09 10 11

Printed in the U.S.A. 23
First Scholastic edition, January 2007

Cover illustration by Brandon Dorman
Text type set in 14-pt. Garamond 3
The display type was set in Dalliance Roman
Book design by Marijka Kostiw

CONTENTS

Prologue

ON HIS NINTH BIRTHDAY, GWYN'S ECCENTRIC GRAND-
mother, Nain, gives him five unusual gifts: a piece of seaweed,
a tin whistle, a Celtic brooch, a small carving of a horse without
ears or a tail, and his sister Bethan's yellow scarf. Bethan disappeared on the moutain behind the family farmhouse four years
previously, and ever since, there has been an "ache of emptiness" in Gwyn's home.

"Time to find out if you are a magician, Gwydion Gwyn,"
Nain tells him.

Gwyn is mystified. Nain says that she believes he has inherited the power of his ancestor, Gwydion, the magician, and if
this is so, Gwyn should use his gifts to get his heart's desire.

Gwyn is skeptical. What should he do with five worn, old
objects?

"Give them to the wind, Gwydion Gwyn, one by one, and
you'll see," says Nain.

Gwyn's longing to find his sister overcomes his reluctance to
act on Nain's advice. He throws the Celtic brooch into the wind
and, in return, a tiny silver spider appears. She has come from

another world to help him find his sister. Gwyn calls the spider Arianwen, the Welsh for "white silver." And in exchange for the whistle, the wind sends him a silver pipe.

Arianwen spins a vast cobweb in Gwyn's room, and he can see a beautiful city in the gossamer, a snowbound city of domed white houses. Children emerge to play in the snow, and the sound of their voices carries into Gwyn's room through the silver pipe. His mother suddenly opens his door and the web is torn; the children and their city vanish.

One dark and icy dawn, Gwyn takes the seaweed and Bethan's scarf out onto the mountain. He lets the wind carry them away, and minutes later, an extraordinary ship appears in the sky. It is covered in ice and when it sails over Gwyn's head, he can see curious flowers and creatures carved on its silver hull. In the ancient myths, Gwydion, the magician, turned seaweed into a ship. Is this the final proof that Gwyn has inherited Gwydion's power? He tells his best friend, Alun Lloyd, about the ship, but Alun is convinced that Gwyn is lying. The two boys gradually grow apart as Gwyn becomes more and more preoccupied with magic.

At school, the other children hear about Gwyn's claim to have seen a "spaceship." They begin to tease him, and the school bully throws a huge snowball at Gwyn's head. Gwyn falls into the snow and finds he cannot get up. A pale-faced girl with white-blond hair appears in the deserted playground. When she comes close, to help Gwyn up, he realizes that he cannot recognize her. She is like his sister, Bethan, only Bethan was dark-haired, her skin tanned by the wind.

Half-afraid of the girl, but longing to know who she really is, Gwyn takes her home.

There is only one gift left for Gwyn to use: the damaged horse. But Nain has warned him that the horse is the one gift he should not give to the wind, for it contains an evil spirit that must never be set free. In a moment of desperation, Gwyn disobeys his grandmother, with dire consequences.

CHAPTER ONE
The Boy from the Chapel

"DON'T GO INTO LLEWELYN'S CHAPEL!" THEY TOLD NIA. "NO good will come of it. Something happened there!" But Nia disobeyed. If she hadn't, nothing would have changed. She'd still be plain Nia, dull Nia, Nia who couldn't do anything!

❄ ❄ ❄

It all began on the day they left Tŷ Llŷr. The children, tucked between boxes in the back of the Land Rover, were waiting for their mother to lock up. Nia was propped up on a rolled mattress at the open end of the car. She was gazing at a red geranium in the kitchen window, the only bright thing left. And then the flower was lifted out of the dark window by unseen hands. It reappeared in the doorway, perched upon a pile of towels in her mother's arms.

"I nearly forgot it!" Mrs. Lloyd beamed over the geranium.

Nia wished she *had* forgotten the flower, just for a day or two. At least there would have been something left alive in Tŷ Llŷr. If a house could look forlorn, then that's how Tŷ Llŷr seemed to her: curtains gone from the windows, the farmyard bare and tidy, and a stillness so unnatural it almost hurt. A stray feather drifted in the sunlight, the only reminder that chickens had once inhabited the yard. It was May but the ewes and their lambs were gone, and the only sounds came from bees in the giant sycamore tree.

Even the children in the Land Rover were silent. Leaving their home had ceased to be an exciting idea; suddenly it had become a rather shocking reality.

Mrs. Lloyd climbed up to sit beside her husband. The engine started. The spell was broken. An excited shouting and chattering broke out.

Nia was the only one to look back and see the boy beneath the sycamore. He was standing so close to the shadowy tree trunk that she could barely make out his shape. But she knew it was Gwyn Griffiths by the mass of dark hair and the way he stood, his hands in his pockets, so very still and thoughtful. No other boy could do that.

Nia nudged her brother, wedged in beside her. "Look, Alun! There's Gwyn!"

There was so much noise, so much movement among the seven children packed tightly together between boxes and cases, that Alun neither felt nor heard Nia, so she raised her own hand and waved, rather tentatively.

The boy beneath the tree responded.

"He's waving, Alun!" Nia shouted above the rumpus.

"What? Who?"

"Gwyn!"

"Oh!"

"He came to say good-bye, Alun! Quick!"

Alun leaned over his sister, accidentally knocking the sheep-dog's nose with his elbow. Fly yelped, the Land Rover lurched around a bend, and Alun was flung backward on top of his twin brothers. Siôn and Gareth were too happy to grumble.

Gwyn Griffiths disappeared from sight.

The Land Rover rattled on down the mountain, gathering speed as the lane became steeper, and the chatter in the back increased to a hysterical crescendo of excitement. Catrin even broke into song.

Mr. Lloyd joined in, humming gustily. He'd done it at last: broken free of the farm that his ailing father-in-law had begged him to take over. Iestyn Lloyd was a small, dark man, his face as weather-tanned as any hill farmer, but he was too fond of his food to stay as fit as he should, too gregarious to enjoy the solitary existence that suited his neighbor Ivor Griffiths so well. But he had tried, no one could say he hadn't. For fifteen years he'd struggled with hard mountain earth, with ewes trapped in snow and lambs lost, and he had failed. He would never make a good farmer — his heart wasn't in it — and with another child on the way, he had to find some way of earning a decent living. When the butcher's shop in Pendewi came up for sale, it was like an answer to Iestyn's prayers. He'd been an apprentice butcher, it was what he knew, what he could do best. He would succeed this time. He'd sold his stock and all his land to Ivor Griffiths, who had a magic touch when it came to animals, and a way of knowing the land that only a born farmer could have.

No one wanted the farmhouse, though. No one wanted

ancient Tŷ Llŷr, with its crumbling chimney, its family of bats, and the plum trees that curled their way under the wavy roof.

"Mae hen wlad fy nhadau yn annwyl i mi," sang Mr. Lloyd, breaking out in a rare exhibition of patriotism, as he cheerfully sped away from the things that Nia loved.

Fly, the sheepdog, rolled her eyes and gazed imploringly at Nia. The dog, at least, felt as apprehensive as she.

There was nothing in Pendewi for Nia. She had neither the talents nor the aspirations of her brothers and sisters. In Pendewi there was a library for Nerys to browse in every day, if she wished. For Catrin, there was a music teacher only two doors away, and a disco on Saturdays. For the boys, there were shops stuffed with comics and bubble gum, with batteries and nails, glue and string. There they would all be, crammed into their little rooms above the shop, reading and singing, building, hammering, and chewing, while the plums turned from green to gold in the orchard at Tŷ Llŷr and strangers put them into baskets and carried them away.

No one would notice the wild Welsh poppies that Nia had nurtured in little places by the stream, or see the white roses behind the farmhouse. The garden would become a carpet of petals, and then, when the wind came, the petals would scatter over the mountain like snow. And no one seemed to care, not even Mrs. Lloyd, preoccupied as she was with thoughts of the baby who would come in summer, when the plums were turning gold.

Gwyn Griffiths's sister had loved flowers, but she had vanished on the mountain. No one knew how this had come about.

"I wish you had waved to Gwyn!" Nia said to Alun, but she spoke half to herself and did not expect him to hear.

The Land Rover slowed down before turning onto the main road. Summer visitors had begun to arrive and the road was busy. Mr. Lloyd swung in behind a camping trailer, and there they stayed, unable to pass the clumsy vehicle, traveling so slowly that Nia could count the primroses on the edge of the road.

At the top of the hill leading down into Pendewi, the trailer stopped without warning. Mr. Lloyd jammed on his brakes and leaned out of the window, mouthing curses about visitors and trailers; he could see the owner in the driver's seat of his smart red car, unconcernedly reading a map. Mr. Lloyd banged his fist on the horn. The children pressed forward, anticipating a fight, all except for Nia, who had noticed something far more interesting.

The Land Rover had stopped beside the old chapel; the chapel that wasn't a chapel now, but a home for someone. The gate and the iron railings had been painted pink and gold, the door was blue with big golden flowers on it, and bright curtains framed the long windows. When Nia stood up she could see down into the room beyond the window. A boy in green trousers lay sprawled across a rug; he was doing something with his hands — making something — but Nia couldn't see what it was. Curious, she leaned farther out, but as she did so, the Land Rover suddenly jerked forward. Nia screamed and clutched wildly at the air, trying to keep her balance.

The boy in the chapel looked up in surprise, and then grinned at Nia's predicament before Alun caught the back of her sweater and pulled her to safety.

"What on earth were you doing?" Nerys, the eldest, inquired irritably. She felt responsible for incidents in the back of the Land Rover.

"I was just looking," Nia replied.

"Looking at what?"

"Just into the chapel. I saw Emlyn Llewelyn from school. I didn't know he lived there!"

"Of course he does," said Alun. "He and his dad. That chapel's a bad place!"

"Who says?"

"Gwyn says!"

"Why?"

"Something happened there," Alun said.

"What happened?" Nia persisted.

"I dunno — something bad! There's something all wrong about that place. No one goes there!"

"It's beautiful!" Nia protested. "And I like Emlyn."

"You don't know, do you?" Alun said in a grim and rather condescending manner.

Nia was silent. Why had she defended Emlyn? She hardly knew him. He was in Alun's class and nearly two years older than she was. She wished she had been able to see farther into his strange home.

Outside Pendewi, the trailer turned left onto the seaside road, and the Land Rover continued on, down into the little market town.

Sunshine flooded High Street. The trees were in blossom, and Saturday shoppers in bright spring clothes bustled in and out of the narrow, gray-tiled houses. *It isn't such a bad place after all,* Nia thought.

The Lloyds parked outside a tall black-and-white building at the farthest end of the town. There was a huge blue van in front of them, with moving company men in gray overalls munching sandwiches in the cab of the truck. The furniture was all in place.

There were two entrances: one that led into a shop furbished with red carcasses and neat trays of sliced meat; the other, a very private-looking black door with a brass number 6 on it.

The family went into their new home through the black, private door, leaving it open to allow warmth and light into the dark house.

Mr. Lloyd persuaded the reluctant and grumbling Fly to go down a long passage to the backyard. Mrs. Lloyd sank into a sunny chair by the door; she was still carrying the red geranium.

The four boys clattered noisily up the stairs and along the creaking and uncarpeted landing, eager to open boxes that had been closed up for weeks — to find ancient and beloved toys and strew them across floorboards of unfamiliar rooms and make the place theirs, their fortress and their home.

Nerys, Nia, and Catrin stood in front of their mother, who was flushed and pretty in her flowery apron.

"Well, I think we should go upstairs first, girls. When the clothes are in the drawers and the beds are made, we'll have a cup of tea."

Nia followed her older sisters upstairs. Nerys and Catrin

disappeared into a room overlooking High Street. Nia glimpsed a wide, sunlit window before the door was closed against her.

Opposite her sisters' room, Siôn, Gareth, and Alun had already extended their territory. A wooden railroad track snaked through their open door and along the landing. Nia sidestepped, but it was too late! She tripped and a red engine flew across the floor.

"Watch it!" the twins sang out. "'Nia Can't Do Nothing!' 'Nia in the Middle!' Nia's got a funny tooth, and her nose goes squiggle, squiggle!"

Nia was fed up with the twins' new rhyme, but she couldn't think of a suitably clever retort. It was all true, of course — that was the worst of it. They'd got her, pinned her down like a butterfly on a board, only she was more of a moth — a very ordinary brown moth who wasn't good at anything except screwing up her nose when she didn't understand something. A moth in the middle, who had two butterfly sisters, an older brother who could fix anything, two younger brothers who could stand on their heads, and an even younger one who got by just because he was the youngest and had curls.

She retrieved the red engine and put it into Siôn's hand. "It's Iolo's engine, anyway," she said.

The twins allowed Nia to escape without further aggravation. She continued down the hall until she reached two open doors at the end. To her left was the bathroom, bright with sunlight and frosted glass. Iolo was playing with something in the tub: Little waves of soapy water were spilling over onto the floor.

Let someone else find the puddle! Leaving Iolo in peace, Nia turned to the room on her right, the room she was to share with Iolo. There were no spaces left for her in her sisters' room and none for Iolo in his brothers'. They would have to put up with each other for the time being. As they had grown in size and number, the Lloyd children had become used to an annual re-arrangement of bedrooms. If the new baby was a girl, Nia would share the baby's bright little room at the top of the house, if it was a boy, Iolo would move in with the new brother, and Nia would stay here in this small, shadowy room that had an old and unused air about it.

The window looked out on to the backyard, a yard in shadow with hardly a blade of grass. There was the river to look at, though, splashing over bleached pebbles beyond the wall enclosing the yard. And on the other side of the river, Morgan the Smithy's long black barn with blue sparks lighting the windows, and Morgan and his sons singing in green coveralls.

Next year, there would be flowers growing by the river. Nia fumbled in her pockets and brought out a tiny paper package. She carefully unfolded the paper and laid on the floor a part of Tŷ Llŷr: honesty seeds in their flat, silvery shells, and tiny black poppy and campion seeds, all mixed together, so that when she sowed them next spring, the meager little patch below would be splashed with orange and purple and pink.

"What's that?" Iolo had finished with boats and stood dripping in the doorway.

"Seeds," Nia replied. "You'd better dry yourself and the floor, or you'll get in trouble."

"I can't find a towel," Iolo explained.

Nia could hear her mother moving around in the room above them. "I'll look downstairs for you. Mom had them in the hall."

"I need something to eat, too," Iolo informed her.

"I'll see."

Nia tucked her precious seeds back into a pocket and went downstairs.

Sunlight was streaming through a semicircle of stained glass above the front door. The hall was lined with a clutter of cases, bags, and upturned chairs, but in the center there was only one thing: a box, *the* box! Nia recognized it; it contained Mom's clothes from twenty years ago: dresses that were too tight but too full of memories to throw away, shoes that were too flimsy, and beads too bright for a mother of seven. It was like a gift, wrapped in the glowing colors from the stained-glass window. A gift for "Nia Can't Do Nothing," who could now become "Nia Can Do Anything"!

Forgetting Iolo and towels, Nia knelt beside the box and began to pick at the string that held it shut. The string fell off and she opened the box. Almost reverently, she began to lift out the contents and lay them on the floor.

There were shouts from above and around Nia, but amazingly, no one came into the hall. Catrin had found the piano and was practicing her scales. Fly was whining somewhere.

"Someone take the dog out!" Mr. Lloyd shouted from the shop.

No one answered.

Nia had found a violet dress, patterned with pink-and-white

flowers. She stood up and slipped it over her head. The hem touched the ground. She knelt again and rummaged around in the box, trying to find the thing she needed. There it was — a wide-brimmed red straw hat. And now she could feel the little paper bundles of beads and shoes at the bottom of the box. She drew out a rope of big silver shells and a pair of pink shoes with stars on them.

Nia kicked off her sneakers and stepped into the pink shoes. The violet dress covered them; she would trip. The silver shells would have to become a belt. They encircled her waist perfectly, not a shell too long. Nia hitched the dress a few inches over the shell belt, just enough to reveal the shoes. She was almost ready.

The finishing touch was a long string of multicolored beads wound once, twice, three times around her neck.

Catrin moved on from Mendelssohn to Mozart, and Fly's distant whine became a long, low howl.

"Someone take that poor dog for a walk," Mrs. Lloyd pleaded from a box-lined room upstairs.

"I'll go," answered Nia.

"Don't let her off the leash, she's not used to the town," came a voice muffled by mounds of linen. "And don't go into any shops."

"I won't!"

"Poor thing! She can't stay here much longer." The rest of Mrs. Lloyd's words were drowned out by Fly's howl of agreement.

Nia tottered down the hall and opened the back door. Four stone steps led down into the yard. Fly was tied to the rail beside the steps, with just enough leash to allow her to stretch out, head on paws, in a tiny patch of sunlight that had managed to creep around the house. The dog leaped up when she saw Nia, and barked joyfully.

"Shhh!" Nia knew her father would not approve of her outfit if he saw her. She began to untie Fly's leash, all the while eyeing the long room that extended into the yard beyond the rest of the house: the hateful room that held all those dead and dreadful things. Through the tiny window she glimpsed a red carcass swinging where her father had just hung it. Mr. Lloyd was whistling, happy among his sides of beef, his lamb chops, and purple pigs' livers. Poor dead, dismembered creatures. It was enough to put a person off meat forever.

"Ugh!" Nia could even smell them.

Fly, free at last, bounded up the back steps and into the house, dragging Nia behind her. They flew down the hall, Fly scattering discarded cardboard and Nia sliding and tripping in the oversize pink shoes.

Nerys appeared at the top of the stairs, alerted by the commotion. "Nia, what are you . . . ?"

But Nia had opened the front door and leaped through it before her sister had time to take in her appearance.

Fly began to live up to her name: Her paws barely touched the ground as she joyfully flew down the street.

The pink shoes hadn't a chance — first one flew off and then the other. Nia didn't dare stop to retrieve them for fear of choking Fly. Clasping the red hat to her head with her free hand, she careered after the dog, darting between startled shoppers and shouts of "Watch it!" "Where are you going, girl?" "What's she doing?"

Not a very favorable first appearance, Nia thought.

Fly bounded on, back toward Tŷ Llŷr and the mountain fields. The road became steeper, and at the end of the town, the dog stopped and stared mournfully up the hill, her sides heaving and her long tongue hanging out like a wet flag.

Nia dropped down beside Fly, in worse shape than the dog. They sat side by side on the hot pavement, gasping and panting. Nia felt as though she'd spent a month in the desert. She closed her eyes and leaned against Fly's woolly neck. When she opened them again a few moments later, she found herself looking at a shop window and at a boy moving past the window and into the shop. He was a tall boy with thick brown-gold hair and green trousers — the boy from the chapel.

Afterward, Nia could never remember whether it was thirst or curiosity that led her to follow him. Whatever it was, she forgot all the rules, all the warnings about sheepdogs in shops, and followed Emlyn Llewelyn through the door.

The wide back of a woman dressed in brown obliterated most of the counter. The wide woman was whispering to the shopkeeper, a man in red suspenders and a grubby shirt, who seemed more interested in gossip than in business. Nia had time to contemplate the rows of sweets and cookies before making a decision. She spied cans of fruit juice on the highest shelf. On the other side of the shop, Emlyn Llewelyn was bending over tubes of glue.

"Yes?" The shopkeeper was staring suspiciously at Nia.

The wide woman had rolled back, propping herself up on the counter; she was staring at Nia's bare feet.

Nia tried to smile but instead screwed up her nose.

"I want a drink, please!" she said quickly.

"Get what you want then. Can you reach?"

"I think so." Nervous of the disapproving glances, Nia thoughtlessly let the loop of Fly's leash slip down her arm and reached for a can of orange juice. Just as her fingertips touched the can, two more customers entered the shop. Fly panicked: She leaped away from the shelves, growling anxiously. Nia was jerked backward, her heel caught in the hem of the violet dress, and she tumbled to the floor, followed by a pile of cans. Suddenly the whole top shelf became possessed. Cans and bottles tottered and clinked and began to roll toward her. There was nothing Nia could do to halt the dreadful and inexorable shower of cans. Some fell on top of her, some crashed to the floor, and others were caught by a darting figure in green trousers. She was aware of the shopkeeper hopping up and down beside her, kicking at the barking Fly and screaming, "Who's going to pay? Look at the shop!" and low voices murmuring, "It shouldn't be allowed!" "She's not wearing shoes!" "And look at the hat!" "What's her mom thinking of?" "Get the dog out!" "No shoes! No shoes!"

And then a boy's voice said, "It isn't a crime, not wearing shoes!" and Emlyn Llewelyn stepped forward, holding Fly tight by the collar. "Only two cans are damaged," he said, "and we'll buy those. Come on!" He tapped Nia on the shoulder and held out his free hand.

Nia looked up. Emlyn had never spoken to her before. He had golden eyes, like a lion.

"Come on!" commanded Emlyn Llewelyn.

Nia put her hand in his, and he helped her to her feet.

"You'd better hold on to your dog," he said, "and pull your dress up or you'll trip again."

Nia obeyed, and Emlyn placed a pile of coins on the counter. Then he strode out of the shop, dragging Nia with him.

"I owe you for the drink," said Nia when the door had been closed against reproachful mutterings.

"That's OK!" Emlyn said. "Are you all right?"

"Yes," Nia lied. Her shins ached where the cans had hit them. "But I'm thirsty."

"Have one on me." Emlyn held out a can. "The dog looks thirsty, too. It's a nice dog. What's its name?"

"Fly," Nia replied, "and it's a she." She opened the can and tipped it to her lips, gulping and coughing as the drink trickled down her throat.

Emlyn watched her for a moment, politely refraining from mentioning the splutters, then asked, "Why don't you bring Fly over to my place and give her a drink?"

"I don't think I'd better," Nia said. "I have to find Mom's shoes. They fell off when I was running, and they've got stars on them."

"OK!" Emlyn accepted her refusal almost too fast, as though he expected it. He kicked the ground with the heel of his sandal and looked away from her.

And suddenly Nia remembered what Alun had said about the chapel: *No one goes there — something happened — something bad!* and she suddenly found herself saying, "All right! I'll come, just for a little while!"

She could see that Emlyn was more than pleased, but trying hard not to show it. "Good!" he said. "Can I take the dog?"

Nia handed him Fly's leash. "I wanted to see the inside of your place," she said.

Emlyn grinned. "I thought I recognized you spying on us. You're Alun's sister, aren't you? You look different in all that stuff. I wasn't sure."

Nia giggled. "I nearly fell out of the car, didn't I?"

"What's going on? Why were you in jeans one minute and then beads and a funny hat the next?"

"We moved," said Nia. "'Moved with the times!' That's what my dad says."

They began to walk up the hill. Fly too hot and thirsty now to run, and Emlyn striding faster than the dog. Nia had to take little running, hopping steps in order to keep up with the boy and to avoid loose stones on the ground.

Once a van passed on the other side of the road, its engine coughing as it strained up the hill, and Fly rushed at it, barking furiously, just as she used to do when strangers passed Tŷ Llŷr.

"She doesn't like cars and that sort of thing," Nia explained breathlessly. "She wants to go home, like me. Only it isn't home anymore — the farm, I mean, where we come from."

"Where did you come from?"

"Tŷ Llŷr, on the mountain. Dad didn't like it, the work was

too rough. Sheep kept dying in the winter, and Mom said the house was too small with another baby coming. But you'd have thought she'd want to stay, since it was her home all her life — she was even born there. Nobody wanted to stay except me and Fly. I planted flowers there. I like to watch things grow and all the colors."

"Are there a lot of you?" Emlyn inquired. He was gazing intently at Fly, and for a moment Nia wondered if he really wanted an answer.

"Seven!" she replied. "Seven children, that is, and I'm in the middle, right in the very middle. Nerys is the oldest, she's clever and quite pretty, but Catrin is beautiful. She called herself 'Kate' last year, she thought it sounded more romantic, but now she's Catrin again. She plays the piano and her hair is — oh . . ." Nia sighed. "All pale yellow and floating, like . . . like ash trees."

Emlyn looked at her with interest but he said nothing, and Nia began to wonder if she'd talked too much. She'd never been able to express herself before, and she couldn't think how it had come about. They walked on in silence until they reached the pink-and-gold railings of the chapel, and all at once Nia began to feel afraid. Fly was apprehensive, too; she kept making worried rumbling noises in her throat.

It was too bright — the painted door, the colored curtains — it was like the house of gingerbread that had tempted Hansel and Gretel, and look what had become of them! *Something happened there, something bad. . . .* Alun's words kept repeating themselves in her head, but Emlyn had taken her hand and was drawing her up the steps to the door!

CHAPTER TWO

A Promise — Broken

THE BLUE DOOR OPENED, AND NIA WAS PITCHED INTO Wonderland. Astonished and enchanted, she forgot her fear and murmured, "Oh! I didn't know! I didn't know!"

From floor to ceiling the walls of the chapel had been covered with bright paintings. Patterns of trees and fields jostled with fantastic flowers, some with faces that Nia knew, and some that she did not. Colored birds swooped through clouds and rainbows, and a boy with gold-brown hair tumbled in the corn, swung from green branches, and slept beside a stream.

"I can see you," said Nia quietly. "You and your life. Who did it?"

"My dad," said Emlyn, not proud, but pleased that she was impressed.

Above her, huge colored butterflies floated on glittering threads from the vaulted ceiling, and all around the room wonderful wooden beasts gazed out with brilliant painted eyes.

"And did he make these?" Nia nodded at the beasts and the butterflies.

"All of it!" Emlyn closed the door. The butterflies shivered in the draft, and the whole ceiling spun and shone.

Was this why everyone avoided the chapel? Just because it was extraordinary? There were no demons here.

Sunlight, pouring through the long windows, dazzled Nia and she didn't dare move for fear of stumbling on a treasure. Something large and dark stooped at the far end of the chapel, but she could not make out what kind of creature it was; its outline was blurred against the glare. And then it began to move. It rose and rose until its long shadow almost touched her feet.

A tall man in black coveralls was approaching; his hair a lion's mane, his eyes golden, like Emlyn's. A large hand clasped Nia's and a deep voice asked, in Welsh, *"Beth ydi'ch enw chi?"*

"Her name is Nia," Emlyn answered for the speechless girl, "and her dog wants a drink!"

"Dog?" Mr. Llewelyn dropped Nia's hand and regarded the bewildered Fly peering around Emlyn's legs. "I told you not to bring dogs in here, boy! He'll wreck my work!"

"I'll take it out, Dad. And it's a *she*. Her name is Fly."

"Fly, is it? Well, remove Fly and give her a drink from the trough."

"Can I let her loose in the field, Dad?"

"Ask the lady," boomed Mr. Llewelyn. "It's her dog."

Nia nodded.

"Let the dog loose, Emlyn. And I will entertain your visitor. Here, lady, have a seat!"

Abandoned by the boy and the dog, Nia perched uncertainly

on the edge of the cane chair that Emlyn's father pulled out for her.

"And now, before tea" — Idris Llewelyn's dark presence loomed over Nia — "may I make a small sketch of you, Nia? So splendid in your beads, and with silver shells all around your waist! And, oh, what a hat!"

Nia had a great desire to run away, but she could not. There was something reassuring about the kindly wooden beasts, the painted landscapes, and the bright butterfly ceiling. So she curled herself tighter into the chair, while Mr. Llewelyn pulled a stool beneath the north window and took up a large sketch pad.

Cocooned in soft cushions, Nia relaxed and let her eyes explore the chapel. In a corner by the door she noticed a trundle bed covered with a striped blanket; Emlyn's place, she decided. There were piles of books under the bed, and beside it, small wooden animals, some perfect and some whose heads and legs were still encased in uncarved blocks of wood. There were empty tubes of glue, pieces of string, scraps of paper, a penknife, and a magnifying glass, but no Legos, no model cars, not a toy of any sort.

At the other end of the chapel, a huge brass bedstead protruded from behind a wicker screen. It was an ancient bed with wonderful knobs and decorations, some scratched and some repainted. Its satin cover was patterned with splashes of red and green and gold, the sort of transport you would need for a very special dream. And then Nia noticed something that made her fingers tighten. Her tiny intake of breath caused Mr. Llewelyn to glance at her face, but he said nothing.

Nia quickly looked away from the thing that had disturbed her, but when the artist looked back at his work, she found herself gazing at the bed again. The hem of the beautiful bed-cover was scarred by a long black mark. Some of the colored threads had been severed at the edge, and hung in uneven, sooty strands. It was a small thing but ugly, and somehow alarming.

She decided to count the piles of rugs that were scattered on the bare floorboards, each one a different size, a different color.

Mr. Llewelyn, a pencil in his mouth, smiled and said, "We've been wanderers, you see. Our collection was gathered from every part of the world, but now we must stay put while Emlyn goes to school."

"And will you go away again, when Emlyn has grown up?" Nia asked.

Mr. Llewelyn was silent for a while, dabbing at his sketch-book, and then he muttered, almost to himself, "Perhaps . . . one day . . ."

Emlyn came in and placed a kettle on a rusty gas stove in a corner. There was an ancient sink beside the stove, with cup-boards above and below it. A teapot appeared, and three blue mugs. *Everything you need in one room,* Nia thought. *Just as it should be.*

"Can we take the tea outside, Dad, to keep Fly company?" Emlyn asked.

"Why not?" said Mr. Llewelyn. He closed his sketchbook and put it on a table beside him. "I'm not showing you yourself yet, Lady with the Violet Dress, because it's not finished. And you must come again, with your hat and your beads."

"I could wear Mom's shoes," said Nia eagerly. "They've got stars on them."

"Why not? Why not?" Mr. Llewelyn laughed, very deep and loud, and helped her out of the chair.

They all went outside and sipped their tea at the back of the chapel, where a steep field of wildflowers stretched down to the river.

"Oh!" cried Nia joyfully. "You can see the mountain from here. You could see Tŷ Llŷr, too, if it wasn't for the trees."

"Ah, that mountain," murmured Mr. Llewelyn. "You know Tŷ Bryn and Emlyn's cousin then?"

"Cousin?" Nia repeated, turning to Emlyn. "Whose cousin are you?"

Emlyn did not reply. He picked up a stick and threw it for Fly.

"Gwyn Griffiths is his cousin," said Mr. Llewelyn. "Their mothers were sisters, but you wouldn't know it. We're down here, and they're on the mountain, and there's a world between us."

They all turned to look at the mountain as he spoke, and in that very second an extraordinary thing happened. A huge, shining cloud appeared from nowhere, right above the mountain, and although the sun still shone, everything went very, very cold, and an icy gust blew Nia's hat onto the grass.

No one referred to the cloud, they just watched it, settling slowly onto the mountain. Emlyn went to fetch a box of cookies. They ate them all except one, which they gave to Fly, who had begun to whine. And Nia became aware that hours — not minutes — had passed. The sun was low, there were shoes to find, explanations to make up. She jumped up, rubbing her cold arms and crying, "I must go. I'll get in trouble!"

"I'll come with you," said Emlyn, grabbing Fly's collar.

"Yes, go with her, boy! And don't forget the hat." Mr. Llewelyn squashed the big hat down over Nia's ears and led them around to the front of the chapel.

As the children passed through the pink-and-gold gate, Mr. Llewelyn exclaimed, "By golly, it's cold! What happened?"

"It's like a spell," said Emlyn, laughing. "Let's run before we turn to stone."

They scampered down the hill, Fly bounding beside them, forgetting where she was going, just happy to be running, and Emlyn shouted breathlessly, "Would your dad sell Fly to me? If I could get the money?"

"Don't know!" Nia called back. "She's a sheepdog, see, and valuable, they say. My dad would want thirty pounds at least. We can't keep her, that's for sure. Anyway, what about your dad?"

"I can talk him into it. I know I can!"

"Oooow!" Nia's bare toes had met something sharp and painful. She sat on the grass and examined her foot. It was extremely dirty, but there was no blood to be seen.

"You all right?" Emlyn crouched beside her.

Fly began to bark.

"No blood," said Nia. "But I think I'll walk now and let the spell get me, if it can."

They sauntered on until they reached the shop where it had all begun. It was closed and the street was empty. Emlyn said,

"I won't come any farther. They might not like it, your mom and dad!"

"Why not?"

"Because they're from the mountain."

"So?"

"I'll tell you one day."

"What were you doing when I looked into the chapel?"

"Making an animal." Emlyn grinned. "That's why I came to the shop — for glue, the tail broke off."

"What sort of animal?"

"It doesn't matter, just an animal. About the dog: I've got some money saved, and I think Dad'll lend me the rest. I'll let you know at school on Monday. Promise not to let them sell Fly till then!"

"I promise," said Nia, never dreaming that she would break her promise.

"Thanks!" Emlyn passed Fly's leash to her and turned to go.

"Emlyn?" Nia had remembered something that had been worrying her. "Where's your mom?"

He stopped and stood quite still with his back to her. Nia thought he wasn't going to reply and wished she hadn't asked the question.

But Emlyn turned, and looking past her at the distant clouds, said, "Mom? She's in the moon, isn't she?" And then he ran back up the hill, only stopping when Nia couldn't reach him, even with a word.

She didn't shout, "That can't be true!" for with Emlyn, she felt anything could be true.

She began to walk down the deserted street, peering in doorways, behind trees, mailboxes, and a telephone booth. The star-spangled shoes were nowhere to be seen.

Ivor Griffiths's Land Rover was parked in the road outside number six, and Nia hoped his presence would occupy her parents' attention while she slipped unnoticed into the house.

But it was not to be.

"Nia Lloyd! What on earth? Where've you been, I'd like to know?" Her mother was in the hall, her face white and angry and her pretty apron covered in dust. "If I didn't know you better I'd have called the police. Nerys went looking and found my best shoes in the gutter!"

"But you don't wear them now," Nia said quietly.

Mrs. Lloyd stamped her foot. "That's not the point, is it?"

Mr. Lloyd emerged from the kitchen mumbling, "What's this? What's this? Close the door, it's gone cold!"

He was closely followed by Ivor Griffiths and three boys with jam on their faces, eager to witness a scolding.

Confined in the dark hall, Fly began to growl.

"Good grief, girl! What d'you think you're doing in that stuff?" Mr. Lloyd seized Fly's leash. "Where've you been, all dressed up like a . . . like a prize cake!"

Iolo and the twins began to giggle, but Nia, lifting her head, said, "I think I look quite nice, really. Anyway, Emlyn Llewelyn's dad thought I did!"

"What? You've been up there?"

"It's beautiful!"

All at once, her parents — and even Ivor Griffiths — began

to chatter low and nervously. They were upset, Nia could feel it. They didn't want to alarm her, but their restraint was far more frightening. Her mother gently removed the red hat and the beads, and started to undo the shell belt, all the while murmuring, "You won't go there again, Love, will you? It's best not to! Promise you won't!"

Nia nodded. She was shivering and wriggling her nose because she didn't understand them, but she was careful not to make a promise. She knew she would go to the chapel again, whatever they said.

"You do as Mom says!" Mr. Griffiths added his advice in a grave and gravelly voice.

Taking her assent for granted, her father and Mr. Griffiths retreated to the kitchen, herding Fly and the boys before them.

Nia stepped out of the violet dress and her mother gathered it up, with the beads and the belt. "I'm going to put these away now, my love," she said, "and I don't want you to wear them again for a bit."

"Even in the house?" Nia asked, dismayed.

"No, your dad doesn't like it!"

"But Mom . . ."

"I'm putting them away," Mrs. Lloyd said firmly. "No more dressing up for a while," and she whisked her bright bundle up the stairs.

"Where are you taking them, Mom?" Nia cried frantically, leaping after her mother, two steps at a time. "I may need them."

"No, you won't!" Her mother was already far above her, on

the narrow stairs that led to the third floor and her own bedroom. "Wash your hands and go and have some tea!"

A door slammed.

Alone on the landing, Nia clenched her fists with frustration and cried, "Oh! Oh! Oh!"

Alun came out of his room, followed by Gwyn Griffiths. "Did you get in trouble?" Alun asked with some sympathy.

"A bit!" said Nia, staring at Gwyn Griffiths. She was surprised to see him so soon after the move from Tŷ Llŷr.

"I came with Dad," Gwyn returned Nia's stare. "To help unpack and stuff."

Nia did not believe him. Upset as she was, she noticed a conspiratorial air about the boys. Gwyn had come to see Alun about something, and it must be very important — and secret.

"Gwyn brought a cake from his mom," Alun said. "It's great! Go and have some!"

Nia was not put off the scent. Something unusual had happened; Gwyn looked so tense. "Come with me!" she said.

Alun was about to refuse, but Gwyn nudged him and said, "We've had our tea and cake, but we'll eat some more," and he led the way downstairs.

Nerys and Catrin were doing the dishes when they went into the kitchen. The dishes had been unpacked but not put away, and they waited in precarious piles around the room.

"You don't deserve cake, Nia Lloyd," said Nerys. "You caused a lot of trouble today. It isn't as if we didn't have enough to do without having to look for you."

"'Nia Can't Do Nothing!' 'Nia in the . . .'" the twins began.

"Now then! Now then!" Mr. Lloyd intervened. "It's all over. Come for some more cake, boys? Sit down, then. By golly, your wife bakes a grand cake, Ivor!"

"She does indeed!" Mr. Griffiths agreed. He wasn't a man given to long speeches, but on the subject of his wife's talent he was always more than generous. "She's a grand cook, Glenys is. She can bake anything, never fails — wins prizes at Pendewi Show every year."

"Every year," Mr. Lloyd repeated on cue.

"And so would our mom if she wasn't washing all day," said loyal Catrin, placing a large slice of sponge cake on Nia's plate. "Aren't you cold just in a T-shirt, Nia? Your arms are blue."

Nia shook her head, her mouth full of cake. She was cold, but cake was more important than cardigans.

"What happened to the weather?" grumbled Mr. Lloyd. "There'll be a frost tonight I bet, and it was so hot today."

If Nia hadn't been looking to see if Alun's slice of cake was larger than her own, she wouldn't have noticed his expression. As it was, she was just in time to see him lift his eyebrows, very slightly, and glance at Gwyn, and she suddenly remembered the terrible cold, nearly two years ago, just after Gwyn had come flying down the lane past Tŷ Llŷr, shouting that he was a magician. No one believed him, of course, and for a while even Alun wouldn't speak to him. And then everything went wrong. A great storm had blown up from nowhere. Sheep had died, and Alun had gotten lost on the mountain, which had disappeared in a cloud of snow. No one could get through. It was a phenomenon they said, but they didn't talk about it much. Alun had been found, and after that, he believed Gwyn. But Nia had always believed, right from the beginning, and when she looked at Gwyn she could feel the excitement in him, half afraid, half yearning, and she knew something would happen again, quite soon.

"I saw your cousin today, Gwyn!" she said brightly.

Gwyn frowned at his plate. "Which cousin?"

"Emlyn Llewelyn," Nia said.

Gwyn looked at his father, who was staring at him. "Who says he's my cousin?"

"Mr. Llewelyn."

"What's so special about seeing Emlyn? He lives here, doesn't he?" Alun said accusingly. Nia got the impression that he was trying to defend Gwyn.

"I just thought . . ."

Before she could finish her sentence, Mrs. Lloyd sang out from the hall, "Bath time, Iolo! Come on!" and bustled in, carrying a bundle of clean clothes.

"Why me first?" Iolo complained, just as he always did.

"You're the youngest! You're the youngest!" the twins chanted, just as they always did.

"Just imagine," said Catrin. "You'll be first in the new bath, Iolo!"

That did it.

"Can we get in, too?" Changing their tune, the twins rushed out after Iolo and their mother, and the room immediately became a little larger.

"We'd better get going, Gwyn." Mr. Griffiths stood up and tapped his son on the shoulder. "We haven't fed the animals."

"I'll get the dog!" said Mr. Lloyd.

Nia thought nothing of her father's words until she heard Fly barking, and then she jumped up, crying, "Dog? You're not taking our dog?!"

"She's a good dog," said Mr. Griffiths, "and not happy here. She'll be better at our place."

"No! No!" Nia ran into the hall. "You never said, Dad. You never told me."

"What's gotten into you, girl?" her father retorted impatiently. Fly was sitting by the door, ready to go, all neat and alert, like someone going to a new school. "Mr. Griffiths agreed to take the dog if I couldn't find another buyer," Mr. Lloyd went on. "She can't stay here. There are no sheep, no field. She'll be so miserable!"

"But I did find a buyer, Dad! I did! I did!"

"And who is that?"

"Emlyn Llewelyn!"

"Don't be silly, Nia! Fly's a sheepdog — a good one, too. She needs sheep and a farm."

"But I promised! I promised!" Nia sobbed. "I can't break my promise, he'll never forgive me."

Through her tears she saw her father pass Fly's leash to Mr. Griffiths. The door opened and the man and the dog stepped out.

Gwyn Griffiths, following his father, looked back, concerned by Nia's outburst. "You can come and see her," he said kindly.

"It's not me that wants to!" Nia snapped.

It wasn't the black door that closed then, it was the bright blue door with golden flowers on it. How could she go back now? They wouldn't want her without the beads and the violet dress. They wouldn't want her without Fly.

"Everything's gone," she wailed at the door, though her words were meant for her family. "I've got nothing left! Nothing, nothing, nothing!"

"Of course you have, my love," said her mother from the stairs. "You've got us and you've got a nice new home!"

Mom didn't understand!

CHAPTER THREE

The Woman in the Moon

"IT WON'T DO, WILL IT, NIA LLOYD?"

Mr. James slammed Nia's exercise book onto her desk. "Do you call that writing? My eyes ache with the searching, searching for a word I can read!"

Nia regarded her messy, unreadable letters. It was the best she could do.

"You'd better buck up, girl, or it's back to kindergarten for you, isn't it?" Mr. James turned away from Nia to silence, with a stare, the snickering that had broken out behind him. He had taken an aspirin to soothe his toothache but any relief he might have expected had been destroyed by the sight of Nia Lloyd's attempt at writing. It was worse than her reading. Was there nothing she could do? Perhaps his long-cherished project would stir some latent talent in the poor girl.

Mr. James, his shoulders significantly braced, his chest puffed out with promise, strolled back to the front of the classroom, where he swung around on his heel, and smiling through swollen gums, delivered his long-awaited announcement.

"And now for the project!" Mr. James exhaled with optimism.

"I want all of you, *all* of you" — he fixed Nia with a cold blue eye — "to do a piece of work about our glorious little patch of Wales, our town and environment. Write a story!" He flourished with his left hand. "Draw a picture, make a painting, compose a song!" Here, several flourishes with his right hand sent papers flying from his desk. Undeterred and in full steam now, Mr. James pounded to a climax. "And at the end of the semester, we'll have an exhibition, a show in the library, for everyone to see."

If she had dared, Nia would have rested her head on her desk in despair. She could already feel the humiliation that was bound to come when her inevitably messy work was exposed to the world. Mr. James was watching her while he rattled on about mountains and monuments, about the Celtic magicians, Gwydion, Math, and Gilfaethwy, and the heroes of Wales. Nia could not listen to his words. She could neither paint nor draw, her writing was a mess, and she had absolutely no musical talent. Why couldn't he leave her in peace?

The bell rang, and she left the classroom with Gwyneth Bowen.

"What are you going to do, Nia?" Gwyneth was excited about the project. There were not many things that Gwyneth could not do. She was Nia's friend, but also her tormentor.

"Don't know," Nia mumbled.

"It's a shame you can't draw," Gwyneth said, as they strolled onto the playground. "It's easier than writing. I'm going to write a story and illustrate it."

"I bet it will be the best," Nia said humbly. "Your work usually is."

"Yes," Gwyneth agreed, "but this time it's going to be fantastic, even for me."

"Well done," Nia said prematurely. She had noticed a boy detach himself from a group and look in her direction. Emlyn Llewelyn was coming toward them. She had an overwhelming desire to flee from the conversation that would end either with her lying, or with Emlyn turning his back on her forever. She wanted so much to talk to him, and she wanted above all to go back to the chapel.

"Hello, Nia!" Emlyn's voice was casual but his eyes were anxious. "Did you talk to your dad?"

"Yes." That, at least, was true!

"What did he say?"

"He . . . he isn't sure."

"What are you talking about?" Gwyneth disapproved of Emlyn — she didn't know why, unless it was because her mother did, or because he didn't go on school trips or wear the special school T-shirt.

"A dog," Nia explained. "Emlyn's going to buy our sheepdog."

"You can't keep a sheepdog," said Gwyneth scornfully. "You don't have any sheep."

"We have a a field," Emlyn said quietly.

"Huh!" Gwyneth sauntered away to join more congenial friends.

"Will you come and see us after school?" Emlyn asked. "Dad wants to finish your portrait — and can you bring Fly?"

"Mom's taken the clothes. She doesn't want me to wear them again."

"Doesn't matter. Just bring the dog!" Emlyn ran off and was lost in the crowded playground before Nia could reply.

She spent the rest of recess alone. She sauntered around the playground perimeter, pausing to gaze at games that did not interest her. Her mind was racing. How could she go to the chapel again? Would Emlyn discover her lie too soon? Would Gwyn Griffiths tell? No, he never spoke to Emlyn. And why was that? Why?

Nia was quite incapable of concentrating on the afternoon activities. Fortunately she was blessed with an hour of singing practice, where she could move her mouth in appropriate directions without making a sound, something that did not require a great deal of effort on her part, for she was, by now, quite skilled at it.

At home her distraction went unnoticed. There was still so much to be done. So many things to fit into new places. The ancient dark furniture, which had seemed so much a part of Tŷ Llŷr, looked awkward and overpowering here. Armoires covered windows, tables protruded through doorways, jam jars mounted the stairs like sentinels — no walk-in pantry here — no room for pickles or plum jam at number six.

The old sideboard seemed to occupy more than half the kitchen. It regarded the family with sadness and disapproval as they sat, squashed in their chairs, beneath its dark brooding presence. But none of them would have been prepared to do without it, for it had been made by Mom's great-great-grandfather Llŷr, one hundred and fifty years ago.

When Nia had helped with the dishes, she informed her mother that she was "going to see Gwyneth for a little while."

"Which Gwyneth?" Mrs. Lloyd inquired.

"Her mom's Mrs. Bowen that sells fabric and buttons and stuff like that," Nia said happily, for this part was all true. "She said I could go and visit anytime. Gwyneth doesn't get along too well with her brother, see, and it'll be nice for her to have company like me!"

"You're not going to the chapel, are you?" Suddenly doubtful, Mrs. Lloyd looked at her daughter.

"Why would I? Fly's gone."

"Go and get your coat then, the evenings are still cool. And don't be long."

Nia dashed up to her room, grabbed her coat from its hook, and ran back to the landing. Here, however, she did not descend the stairs, but slipped off her shoes and tiptoed up to the third floor. The door, which stood open before her, revealed a room bursting with boxes: the new nursery, waiting to be decorated. Nia opened the second door and peeped into her parents' room. It was filled with their enormous bed. How the bed had reached its lofty, inaccessible position she could not imagine, but there it was, huge and magnificent, with its patterned posts and patchwork cover, taking up all but a few inches between the closet and the wall. If she stood on the bed she would be able to reach the tiny scrap of violet that her mother had failed to conceal behind a row of jars on the top shelf of the wardrobe.

Nia withdrew her head and listened to the house: Catrin practicing scales in the front room; the boys making explosive noises in the throes of a war game; her parents watching television in the kitchen. Nerys had gone to the library, which was open late on Mondays. There was no one to spy on Nia.

She leaped up onto the big bed and stretched upward. A jar wobbled dangerously and then was still. Nia extended two fingers between the jars; she could feel a piece of material. She gave a little tug; the jars rattled. She tugged again, very gently, and the violet dress slithered past the jars and dropped onto her head.

Nia jumped off the bed and thrust the dress inside her coat, which she zipped up to her neck. Then she half ran, half slithered down the steep and shiny wooden staircase. Pausing on the landing to step into her shoes, she confidently tiptoed down the second flight of stairs.

She was about to open the front door when her father came out of the kitchen. "You still here, girl?" he asked, glancing out of the kitchen at her bulging coat.

"Couldn't find my coat," Nia answered.

"Don't go into Llewelyn's chapel, girl," Mr. Lloyd said earnestly. "No good will come of it."

"But why, Dad? What's the matter with it?" Nia had to ask.

"Something happened there."

Before Nia could question him further, Mr. Lloyd escaped into his shop.

She opened the front door and stepped out into the quiet street. Bowen's Fabric Shop was only three doors away, next to the house where tiny Miss Olwen Oliver turned truants into choirboys, and skinny girls into stars of the opera. Nia decided she would visit Gwyneth, just for a moment, so that if she was questioned later, she could truthfully answer that she had seen her friend.

Gwyneth was not at home, and there was no answer to Nia's insistent knocking. She would have to risk a lie.

There was a light in the chapel, but Nia's first timid knock went unheard, and reluctant to intrude, she climbed onto the lowest rung of the pink-and-gold railing and peeped into the window. Emlyn was kneeling on the floor beside an oil lamp; he was absorbed in one of his animals, in an attitude of such stillness he might have been a statue himself. The only movement came from a small knife in his hand, which flashed now and then in the lamplight. Mr. Llewelyn was nowhere to be seen.

Nia stepped down from the railing, climbed the steps that led to the blue door, and knocked again. The door was opened a few seconds later by Emlyn. He seemed pleased to see her. "What did your dad say about the dog?" he asked.

"He's thinking about it."

"Good." Emlyn held the door wider to let her pass.

Nia looked uncertainly at the figure hunched by a window before his easel.

"Don't worry about him," Emlyn led her in and closed the door. "He's in a bad mood. Work's not going well." He spoke as though his father were not aware of them.

Nia decided to adopt Emlyn's attitude. "What's he painting?"

"I don't know — patterns. Someone commissioned it,

someone from London. So we'll have a feast when it's finished. They're paying a thousand pounds. I'll get new sneakers."

Nia regarded the worn straps of leather stretched across Emlyn's bare toes. She had thought that he wore sandals by choice. "Will you have roast beef for your feast?" she asked. "There's beef hanging in our place, and pigs, all slit open with the blood dripping out."

A look of horror passed over Emlyn's face. Nia realized how grim her words must have sounded. She hadn't meant to shock him; she just wanted to voice her disapproval of Mr. Lloyd's new trade.

"We don't eat meat!" Emlyn said.

"I don't like it, either," Nia said quickly. "It smells," she added for good measure. "But I have to eat it because my dad's a butcher"

Emlyn looked relieved. Nia could not be held responsible for the food that was forced upon her.

"*Pwy sydd yna?*" The Welsh words came low and weary through the darkening chapel. Nia had almost forgotten about Mr. Llewelyn.

"It's Nia!" Emlyn said. "The girl with the dog." He crouched back onto the floor and picked up his knife.

"*Ble mae'r ci?* Where is the dog?"

"I — I couldn't bring her today," Nia grasped for words that would not utterly condemn her when her lies were discovered.

"And where are the pink shoes with stardust on them that you promised to wear?" Mr. Llewelyn's dark features were not fierce. He seemed more like a tired but kindly beast, ambling toward her through his jungle of exotic animals.

"Mom hid them," Nia said, "and the hat and the beads. I brought the dress, though." She unzipped her coat and proudly displayed her loot.

"It's too dark now," Emlyn's father sighed and looked over her head. "What a sky. It's like slate."

They don't want me, Nia thought. *They don't need me without the dog. The dress is not enough.*

"Have some soup. It's ready." Emlyn, absorbed in his carving, seemed to make the invitation as a matter of course, rather than a genuine desire for her company.

Undeterred by his indifference, Nia said, "Yes, please!" And just in case she seemed too eager, "I didn't have much at dinner."

Mr. Llewelyn went to the stove and ladled out three bowls of soup. It was hot and thick — and rather too green for Nia's liking — but she decided she could get used to it.

They sat cross-legged on the floor to eat their soup, even Mr. Llewelyn, and it didn't matter that no one spoke. They didn't grasp for words, search for a subject with which to entertain one another. Nia felt so comfortable in the silence that she began to wonder at her contentment, and in wondering, broke the spell and remembered the project. She began to cough and couldn't stop until Mr. Llewelyn patted her on the back. Even then she still gulped for air, red in the face and breathless.

"Hold on, girl. I'll get you some water!" Emlyn's father went to the sink.

"It isn't just the soup, is it?" Emlyn looked hard at her. "Something came into your mind to spoil the taste. It does that with me, sometimes. What was the thing that made you cough?"

Nia sipped the water that was handed to her, and while Mr. Llewelyn knelt to give them slices of coarse brown bread, she said, "It's the project, Mr. James's project!" And with a sigh, she unburdened herself and told her hosts about all her problems with Mr. James and his desire to exhibit the classroom's work on their environment.

"He's a real pain, that Mr. James," Emlyn remarked sympathetically. "He's always going on about exhibitions. He won't leave you alone. I'm glad I'm in Miss Powell's class now."

"I'm hopeless," said Nia wistfully. "They'll all laugh at whatever I do. 'Nia Can't Do Nothing,' that's what my brothers call me."

Mr. Llewelyn threw back his head and roared with laughter.

"It's not funny," Nia said, offended.

"It is, you know." Mr. Llewelyn was still chuckling, but seeing the children's reproachful glances added, "It's not you, though, Nia. It doesn't make sense, you see, 'Nia Can't Do Nothing.' If Nia *can't* do nothing, then Nia *can* do something, see?"

Nia thought she saw, but knowing that her brothers used bad grammar didn't solve her problem.

And then Emlyn repeated, "'Nia *Can* Do Something.' Everyone can do something!"

"Not me!" Nia said gloomily.

"Don't be so pessimistic. You grow flowers, you said. You can see colors, feel them. I know you can."

"What do you do at home, girl?" asked Mr. Llewelyn, inspired by his son's enthusiasm. "Can you knit or make things? What do you do to help your mom?"

"I mend the socks," Nia said doubtfully. "I'm quite good at that, actually!"

"There you are then," said Mr. Llewelyn. "Sew a picture, make fields and mountains from cloth and cotton."

"Something silver for the river — maybe tinsel — and wool for the clouds," Emlyn went on eagerly.

"And flowers," said Nia. "Mom's got bright yellow dust cloths, and old sheets cut up for rags, but still white as anything. Maybe I can do it."

"Of course you can, girl. You've got imagination." Mr. Llewelyn leaped to his feet and gathered up their empty soup bowls. "I'll find you a piece of canvas big enough for a masterpiece, and you can sew your shapes onto it."

He put the bowls in the sink and began to search among the empty frames and unfinished paintings that leaned against the wall. Suddenly, in the shifting and searching, one of Emlyn's paintings appeared. Nia found herself looking at a woman hanging in the moon; not hanging, perhaps, but stretching up against the lower half of a crescent, as someone might do when clinging to a fairground creature on a carousel. Her hair was black, and her long, pale dress floated out and around the moon like a cloud. Nia knew who it was, but all the same she asked, "Who is that?"

And Emlyn answered, as she knew he would, "It's my mom!"

"Did you paint it?"

"Yes, I did; after she left, two years ago."

Nia wanted to ask about the moon and why the woman was hanging there, but the painting vanished under another painting and Mr. Llewelyn stepped toward them with a long roll of something. He held one end and unfurled six feet of dusty canvas, filling the air with tiny lamplit particles that glowed and drifted around their heads.

"Here it is then — the background for your picture, Nia." Mr. Llewelyn laid the canvas beside her and stepped away.

"But it's so big!" Nia exclaimed.

"A masterpiece must be large," he replied. "I have a feeling about this canvas," Emlyn's father went on. "I think you will find yourself here. But keep it out of sight until it is complete. It must be yours, all yours. If you need help, ask us — no one else. And one day, we will see here the true and special Nia!"

"Thank you!" Nia stood up and stared uncertainly at the huge rectangle at her feet.

"Well, take it, girl!" commanded Idris Llewelyn. "Roll it up and hide it under your coat."

"But the dress — I can't hide them both in my coat."

"Leave the dress here," Emlyn suggested, "and get it when you bring the dog. Will it be soon?"

"I suppose so." Nia wished he hadn't mentioned Fly. She was taking their gift under false pretenses. She knelt and folded the canvas, tucking it guiltily into her coat, like a thief who knows he has been seen but has gone too far to save himself.

"You look so glum, girl," Mr. Llewelyn remarked. "Cheer up! This is the beginning. Can you use an iron?"

Nia nodded and got to her feet.

"Iron the creases out of your canvas when no one is around, and then hide it."

"I'll do that," said Nia. "I'd better go now, and thank you for the soup and . . . and everything."

"Drat the sky!" Mr. Llewelyn was once again preoccupied with his own work. "The light is going and I should have had another two hours."

Emlyn followed Nia out of the chapel and began to accompany her down the hill.

"I'll be all right," Nia said.

"I'll come anyway," he replied and fell into step beside her.

"What's your mom's name?" Nia asked, hoping to forestall any inquiries about Fly.

"Elinor," he said.

"That's a beautiful name. Why do you think she's in the moon?"

"She told me!"

And then, without any prompting, Emlyn began to tell Nia of the night his mother left — of the howling wind that tore shingles from the chapel roof and sent them banging against the windows, the baby crying and his father roaring in the dark because there were no lights. "But I could see them both," Emlyn said softly. "The moon was so bright and my mom was walking up and down and around the wooden animals, pushing at them, like she hated them. I fell asleep while they were still fighting, and then, much later, she woke me. She said she was taking the baby and leaving my dad. She wanted me to go with her, but I said no. I couldn't leave my dad. And then she said something: '. . . *Yr Hanner Lleuad,*' the half moon, that's all I heard because of the wind. So I painted her in the moon — in a crescent moon — because that's what she said. But I never told my dad why and he never asked."

They were no longer walking, but now and again placing one foot in front of the other until, at last, they stopped moving altogether and Nia said, "She just left, like that, in the middle of the night?"

"She just left," he replied.

Nia felt he had left something out, perhaps the most important thing of all, but she had no right to ask any more questions, for she had broken her promise, and even now, when she knew he had probably confided more to her than to anyone, she could not bring herself to tell him the truth about Fly.

The sky was, indeed, like slate: Heavy and damp, it pressed all around them, holding the shape of fields and mountains fixed and dark in the distance. Emlyn looked away to a lamplit window at the top of the hill. "I stood on my bed after she left," he said, "and I looked out of the window. There was a Land Rover on the road, and a man beside it."

Nia gasped. "Do you know who it was?" she asked.

"Yes," said Emlyn. "I knew him all right. It was Mr. Griffiths, Gwyn's dad. He took my mother away."

Nia looked hard into his eyes, willing him to smile and tell her that it was not so — not Gwyn's father — but the gaze he steadfastly returned was so grave and so sad that she had to believe him. And then, all at once, he burst out, "They blame him — blame my dad for driving my mom away. But it's all a lie. She chose to leave. She didn't have to go. My dad gave her a home with pictures on the wall and a butterfly ceiling for her baby. She didn't have to go. And they blame me, too, for staying. 'A boy should go with his mother,' they said, but I couldn't, could I? I couldn't leave my dad."

Emlyn, who had seemed so confident, was shaking his head from side to side like a sleepless child, and Nia knew that her answer really mattered. Could she manage, just for once, to get it right? "No," she said calmly, "you couldn't leave your dad — he'd be alone."

Emlyn smiled almost apologetically, and Nia knew that she had chosen her words wisely.

"I'll come all the way with you tonight," Emlyn said. "There are ghosts in the air."

They laughed and then they ran — ran all the way to number six, where Emlyn held his nose and made hideous faces at the butcher's dark and empty window, and Nia giggled as she rang the bell. Someone had locked the door. Nerys opened it with a book in one hand. "I saw your friend Gwyneth in the library," she said.

"Yes, her dad let me in and I waited!" Nia decided that Gwyneth's father was not likely to frequent libraries. "We had a great time. Gwyneth's got a new dollhouse."

"She's spoiled," said Nerys. Her glasses had slipped to the end of her nose and she didn't see Emlyn, dancing in the street, thumbs in his ears and feet turned out like Charlie Chaplin. "What're you grinning at?"

"Nothing," Nia replied. She followed her sister into the house and turned to give Emlyn a secret signal of farewell.

Emlyn had stopped dancing. He was staring into the hall, listening to the cheerful sounds beyond — the singing, shouting, and laughter. He reminded Nia of a hungry, golden-eyed animal, searching for warmth.

She hated closing the door.

CHAPTER FOUR

A Fight

IT WAS A COLD NIGHT. THE GRAY CLOUDS DRIFTED SOUTH and the moon sailed out bright and startling from behind the mountains. Falling through frosted glass, it filled the yellow bathroom with soft light, and Nia, sleepless with impatience, knew that she had found a safe and secret place to do her work.

Iolo was not easily disturbed from sleep, his face was pressed against his blue monster and his breathing was calm and even as his sister crawled beneath her bed to retrieve the canvas from its hiding place. Nevertheless, she tiptoed through the door and dared not shut it too harshly behind her.

In the bathroom, in the brightest patch of moonlight, Nia spread her canvas and gazed at it. She had managed to iron it in the tiny upstairs room, on the board her mother had left unattended while she ran Iolo's bath. Nia stroked the rough surface and closed her eyes tightly, silently demanding the canvas to show her where and how to begin. A huge rectangle of dull brown stared back at her, giving no advice, no encouragement.

Once again, the hateful and familiar feeling of hopelessness began to overwhelm Nia. She sank back on her heels, numb with disappointment. She was not what they thought after all. She could not see shapes and colors where they did not exist. She was not gifted with imagination. The Llewelyns had burdened her with a talent she did not possess. They expected too much.

Motionless, she crouched on the cold floor until the church clock struck twice. The lonely, hollow sound made her shiver. It was time to put away the masterpiece that would never be.

A wisp of cloud passed across the moon: the long dress of a lady in the sky. A shadow covered the canvas like a ghost, and when it had gone, a faint shape appeared beside Nia's cold hand where it touched the frayed edge. The pale form gathered strength and color, becoming a roof, dark gray, with a chimney in the center. Another roof emerged beside the first. This one was dark red with a curl of smoke drifting from the chimney. The lower edge of the canvas began to fill with imaginary shapes and colors. Nia was so excited she ran to the bedroom, crashing the door back against Iolo's toy box. The rhythm of her brother's quiet breathing changed, but he did not wake.

Nia opened a dresser drawer and took out her sewing basket. She found a large needle, scissors, and a ball of soft gray wool. Terrified that the picture in her mind would evaporate before she could commit it to canvas, she rushed back to the bathroom, slipped on the shiny floor, and crashed into a stool, sending it spinning into the bathtub. In the silent house, the noise seemed deafening. For a whole minute Nia waited, frozen, against the wall. When she had assured herself that she had not woken her family, she knelt beside her canvas and began to thread the needle. This done, she made three tiny stitches in the material. She paused to consider, then made a long stitch, then a curve. Nia teased the wool with the sharp end of her needle, and pale gray, drifting smoke appeared.

"Oh!" she sighed, surprised and delighted by her achievement.

"Nia?"

Someone had been disturbed after all. Catrin stood in the open doorway.

"Can't you sleep?"

It was too late to hide the canvas. "Something woke me!" Nia said.

"What's that on the floor?"

"Nothing — just a piece of stuff I found. I'm . . . I'm sewing on it. Please don't tell."

"I won't tell, but you'd better go to bed now or you'll never wake up in the morning." Kind Catrin never scolded.

Nia smiled and rolled up her work. She had begun. Nothing mattered now. The smoke was there and it would remain. Tomorrow there would be a chimney and a roof and perhaps pink blossoms on a tree. "I'll sleep now," she said happily.

Catrin followed Nia to her room and smoothed the pillow. "You're a funny one," she said as Nia climbed into bed.

"I'm glad it wasn't Nerys who found me," Nia whispered.

"I bet you are!" Catrin began to tidy the rumpled sheets. Before she had finished, Nia was asleep.

❊ ❊ ❊

There began a week of feverish activity for Nia. Scraps of cotton, corduroy, and velvet were begged from her mother and retrieved from rag bags, boxes, and bottom drawers. Christmas paper, tinsel, and ribbons were carefully acquired from friends and neighbors. Gwyneth Bowen was very generous and donated a whole box of shop-soiled wool and her mother's tired satin petticoat. She didn't even ask what they were for.

All these precious pieces Nia hoarded, mouselike, in plastic bags beneath her bed. And no one guessed, no one asked, no one wanted to know what she was up to!

Luckily Mrs. Lloyd had never been a great one for tidying bedrooms, and the hoard grew, undisturbed, until there was scarcely enough room for the canvas which Nia rolled with great care every night after she had smoothed bits of material, snipped loose threads, and ensured that the glue was dry.

She forgot about Fly and her broken promise. Her mind was filled with the color and complexion of the world around her: the intensity of shadows, shades of the sky, the brilliance of flowers, and curving shapes of trees. She was completely enthralled by her new occupation, though she managed to chat with Gwyneth and play hopscotch while counting windows.

And then one day, when the canvas lay safe and secret under her bed, already half filled with patches, Nia was forced to remember Fly. She was standing in the middle of the playground, gazing up through half-closed eyes, at a giant evergreen in the churchyard beyond the school wall.

She was hardly aware of the activity around her, until someone began to approach and Emlyn Llewelyn broke through a hazy foreground.

I can ask him about the evergreen, she thought. *He'll know if it's green or black.* But when she had made sense of his expression she realized that she could ask him nothing. He had discovered her lie.

When he knew he had Nia's attention, Emlyn stood very still, his golden eyes dangerous and his words quiet and cold.

"Why didn't you tell me about the dog?"

"I didn't know . . . I wasn't sure, I . . . I couldn't . . ."

"You promised!"

Nia shook her head hopelessly. "My dad did it. I told him about . . . about you wanting the dog and all, but it was too late!"

"You let them have it and you never told me!" Emlyn's voice began to rise.

A crowd of children, sensing conflict, gathered closer.

"Why Gwyn Griffiths? Why not me? You knew I wanted the dog. You knew how much I wanted her."

Nia looked away from him. She had been prepared for anger; it was his humiliation that she could not endure.

"Look at me," Emlyn cried and, turning, Nia saw his hand go to his pocket and pull out a strip of leather. "I even bought a leash. Stupid, wasn't it? A leash and no dog. I don't need it now, do I?"

Emlyn raised his arm. For a moment the strip of leather hung innocently from his hand, and then suddenly, it came snaking toward Nia as she stood awaiting her punishment.

But someone stepped in front of her, and Nia heard gasps of horror and delight as the hard leather struck Gwyn Griffiths in the face. An angry red mark appeared on his cheek and he walked toward Emlyn, holding the leash tight in his hand.

Emlyn stood his ground for a moment, angry and unrepentant, then he turned and ran.

Gwyn pursued him slowly at first, but as Emlyn approached the low playground wall, Gwyn gathered speed. Emlyn flung himself at the wall and tumbled over into the narrow lane between the churchyard and the playground. Gwyn followed only seconds after, and Nia found that she was running, too, knowing that whatever was going to happen would be her fault.

"Nia Lloyd, where are you going?" called Miss Powell, on duty by the jungle gym and more concerned with death-defying five-year-olds than Nia Lloyd's flight. She hadn't even noticed the boys.

"You'll get it when you get back!" someone called as Nia fell, breathless, into the stony lane.

She caught sight of Gwyn turning onto the path that led to the churchyard and stumbled after him. Her mind was racing her feet, which would not obey her. She could not keep her balance; twice she tripped and crashed onto the stones. "You'll get it!" warned the singsong voices, Gwyneth Bowen's louder than the rest.

Nia reached a swinging wrought-iron gate. The voices faded. She hesitated. Beyond lay the graveyard, which was not her favorite place. It was dark with ancient trees; a place where long ago, before any church was built, men had prayed to gods other than the one she knew.

She braced herself and passed through the gate. A shroud of trees enveloped her as she walked down the lane, soft with moss and weeds. She watched and listened for signs of battle, but there were none. Perhaps the two boys had parted without a fight, yet she could not believe it.

There were five evergreens in the churchyard, all of them a thousand years old, so it was said, and Nia could believe it. Their hollow trunks were scarred and dusty, their branches of dark needles bent and cracked. Mysterious trees, sacred and poisonous.

She left the path and allowed herself to be drawn farther out into the maze of older graves, into a place inhabited by phantoms whose names could not be read, and where the yews trailed damp fingers over decaying stones. The feeling of unseen and mysterious power never left her, and she wondered why Emlyn had chosen such a retreat.

On a patch of dead ground, beneath the farthest, darkest tree, Nia saw the boys. Or rather she saw one form, circling slowly. They were closed in combat, their tangled arms embracing, their legs hardly moving. The black head tight against the brown and their bodies constantly pushing unremittingly, one against the other. And then one boy broke free — Emlyn — and he began to beat his adversary with desperate and deadly fists.

Gwyn reeled back, defending himself with raised arms. Emlyn was the taller and more powerful boy, but Nia sensed a strength about Gwyn that could withstand and even overcome the other. And she remembered that strange time two years ago, when Gwyn had inflicted a terrible injury on fat Dewi Davis. No one knew how he had done it. They said a stone had been thrown and broken Dewi's nose, but Nia hadn't seen a stone: She believed Gwyn had a power that could not be named. Once, he had called himself a magician.

The magician was kneeling now, shielding his head with his hands. Emlyn seized him by the shoulders and would have thrown him over, but something happened. The kneeling boy seemed to lose his shape or change it.

Emlyn stepped back, his eyes fixed on Gwyn, utterly astonished. He kept on stepping back until he was almost lost in the gloom beneath the tree. When he stopped moving, the two boys were frozen in a great bowl of nothingness where no birds sang, no leaves fell, and even dust was motionless. And Nia was standing on the very edge, breathing, but only just. She wanted to scream, but something was strangling all sound.

Then Gwyn stood up, his arms raised, fingers stretched wide, like a cat spreading its claws. A boy who was not a boy, but a part of the magic in the sacred trees and of the ageless shadows beneath them. All the dark power that still dwelled in the graveyard seemed to have gathered into his hands.

And then he let it go. His arms dropped to his sides, and something fell away from him, an unseen mantle that he had borrowed from the air in a moment of need.

Emlyn, released, sprang forward and felled his enemy with one blow.

He ran past Nia, scarcely seeing her. The victor. But his face showed repentance and when he reached the path, she thought she heard a sob.

Gwyn got to his feet, rubbing his head. An ordinary boy who

had been hurt, but Nia still felt in awe of him. She walked toward him, meaning to thank him for defending her, but instead she asked, "Why did you let him beat you?"

"He's stronger," Gwyn said.

"No he isn't! You can do things to the air. It's frightening!"

Gwyn gave her a sly look, the sort of look he usually reserved for Alun. She felt privileged.

"Emlyn had to win," was all he said.

Nia understood. "He is your cousin, isn't he?" She looked sideways at him.

Gwyn sighed. "Yes, he's my cousin. But he hates me, and it isn't just the dog." He closed his eyes and rubbed his forehead. "There's something wrong between our families."

"Your father stole his mother," Nia said quietly.

"That's not true!" He sounded angry, but astonished at the solution to an old and painful puzzle. "It can't be true. . . ." His voice trailed off and then he added softly, "I didn't know. Why didn't he tell me?" Then he said again, "It's not true!"

Nia was glad that he hadn't known, hadn't been part of the plot. "It is true," she said. "The way Emlyn told it to me. . . . He couldn't have made it up!"

They began to walk toward the church, their feet making no sound on the damp evergreen needles.

"My dad's secretive," Gwyn murmured. "He's deep, but he always has a reason. Where did he take Emlyn's mom then?"

"Emlyn says she's in the moon."

Gwyn didn't laugh, he just said, "She was my auntie Elinor. She was beautiful and very special to Bethan."

"Your sister?"

"Yes. She left . . ."

Nia thought he was going to tell her where, but he continued, ". . . nearly five years ago. Disappeared. And then my auntie Elinor," Gwyn was almost speaking to himself. "They'd just come back from somewhere, the Llewelyns — France, I think it was. Emlyn was born over there, I didn't know him. Bethan really took to Elinor — they used to plant seeds together and pick wildflowers and press them in a book. Then, in November, Bethan left. We didn't see much of the Llewelyns after that. Dad was . . . well . . . sick or something. And soon after, Auntie Elinor went away, and Dad told me my uncle Idris was wicked and I was never to speak to him or Emlyn again, they weren't relatives anymore."

"Emlyn isn't wicked!" Nia said.

Gwyn shrugged. "I've gone to the same school," he said, "and I've sat in the same room, and since then I've never spoken to him till today."

"Did you speak today?"

Gwyn frowned. "No," he said, surprised by his answer. "But we fought and that's like speaking, in a way."

"It was my fault, all of it!" Nia said.

"No it wasn't. I had to defend you, and myself. I had to pay him back for being mad, he expected it."

They were on the path now, and leaving the trees. The playground was near but unusually quiet. They had almost reached the churchyard gate when Nia found the courage to ask, "Gwyn, you told us once that you were a magician. Are you one?"

He sighed, thrust his hands deep into his pockets, and looked up at the sky. "Yes," he said, "but don't talk about it. It's not always an advantage, being a magician! I have to hide it. It's getting stronger in me, and sometimes I'm afraid I'll get it wrong; do something, in a moment, without thinking, and then . . . !"

Fearing he had said too much, Gwyn waited for a scornful response. None came. Remembering what had happened beneath the tree, Nia was amazed, and did not know what to say. But instinct told her that Gwyn's power would never hurt Emlyn again.

Beside the gate they saw the dog's leash, where Gwyn had dropped it. He picked it up. "What should I do with this?" he muttered.

"Keep it," Nia said. "Maybe you can give it back one day."

Gwyn put the leash in his pocket. "Fly might have pups," he said thoughtfully.

They emerged into sunlight, and Nia saw clearly the red stripe across Gwyn's cheek where the leather had lashed it.

"Does your face hurt?" she asked.

"Not much."

"What are you going to say about the mark?"

"I'll say I had a fight with Nia Lloyd, and she beat me!" He laughed and then he ran down the lane away from her.

They soon discovered why the playground was so quiet. In spite of Miss Powell's vigilance, the jungle gym had claimed a victim: One of the Lloyd twins, Gareth, lay moaning on the ground.

CHAPTER FIVE

The Curtain

IOLO RUSHED TO NIA WHEN HE SAW HER. "WHERE'VE YOU been? I wanted you. Gareth's hurt!" he cried.

Before Nia could reply, Siôn was pulling at her skirt and yelling, "Where've you been? Gareth's had an accident!"

"I can see that," Nia said sharply. "I wasn't far away — I'm here now. What happened?"

"He was balancing," Siôn said proudly. "It was great. He was right on top! Miss Powell yelled at him to come down. He'd have been all right if she hadn't yelled."

Miss Powell was in a bit of a state. She seemed unable to decide whether to scold, comfort, or assist the stricken boy. Then Mr. James arrived and took control of the situation. He gently felt all of Gareth's limbs, picked him up, and carried him into the school.

A crowd of children respectfully made way for the patient's relatives. Alun, Nia, Siôn, and Iolo, wearing suitably funereal expressions, followed Mr. James and their brother. Nia wished that Nerys and Catrin were with them and not a half mile away at the high school.

Dr. Vaughan arrived and only minutes later, Mrs. Lloyd. Gareth was whisked off to the hospital, accompanied by his mother. The other Lloyds returned to their separate classrooms, amid sympathetic murmurs from their friends.

"Is it fatal?" Gwyneth inquired in a solemn whisper.

Nia did not deign to reply.

The anxiety that she betrayed when she returned home was misinterpreted by her mother.

Mrs. Lloyd had left the hospital, reassured that broken bones were all the rage for eight-year-old boys.

"Don't fret, Dear. It's only a broken leg. It'll soon heal," she said when Nia, tears springing to her eyes, had misplaced a glass and let it smash onto the tiled kitchen floor.

Nia felt guilty. Her thoughts were not with Gareth. Emlyn hadn't returned to school that afternoon. Where had he gone and why? He had won a fight, but she could not forget the desolate look on his face when he had passed her, and she could not forget the way Gwyn Griffiths had frozen life in the dim space under the evergreens, or the red mark on his cheek that should have been on hers.

When she took her canvas to the bathroom that night, there was no moon. The streetlamp was bright enough, but her picture looked somehow dead in artificial light. She found green corduroy for the evergreen trees, but couldn't remember their shape, and there was not enough of Alun's old gray socks to make a church.

"I can't do it! I can't do it!" she muttered angrily at the canvas. "Nia can't do nothing," who had been absent for a week, was peering over her shoulder, clutching at her hands. She needed to see Emlyn and his father, to ask for their advice and encouragement. Would they ever speak to her again?

When she replaced the canvas under her bed she had not added one stitch to it. Nor did she add any the following night. Emlyn had not been in school.

On the third evening after Gareth's accident, Nia slipped into the boys' bedroom when it was empty, and took a new gray sock from Gareth's drawer.

"He'll only need one now," she told herself.

That night she tried to cut it into the shape of a church. The frayed pieces stretched and fell apart. Nia sat in the bathroom, glaring at her unfinished collage, remembering that Gareth had not lost a leg but merely broken one. She snipped the gray sock into tiny shreds and flushed them down the toilet.

"There's something in the toilet," Nerys complained the next morning at breakfast. "It's gray and it won't flush."

"Worms!" said Siôn with relish.

"You're a worm, worm!" Nerys retorted.

"It's a rag — just a rag," Nia said quickly. "All cut up."

"Oh Nia!" Mrs. Lloyd, distracted from scraping burnt toast into the trash can, slipped, causing sooty crumbs to fly everywhere. "Now look what you've made me do. I've told you not to flush things down the toilet."

Nia wondered if there'd be a hole in the toast after her mother's attack. "I thought it would go down if I cut it up," she said meekly.

"Now then, girl. You know better than that. We don't need

trouble with the pipes again," said Mr. Lloyd, scrubbing his butcher's fingers extra hygienically in the sink.

❄ ❄ ❄

Emlyn was in school for the first time since the fight. He wouldn't even look in Nia's direction.

She decided to postpone making the church and concentrate on trees, but she didn't know how to make blossoms. And then she remembered something.

Catrin had a music lesson after school that evening, with Miss Olwen Oliver (who was always called "Olwen" to distinguish her from her sister, Enid Oliver, who ran the bakery and took boarders).

"Can I come with you to Miss Olwen Oliver's?" Nia asked her sister.

"Whatever for?"

"I like listening to you play."

Nia had tried music lessons but had proved "unmusical," as Miss Oliver put it.

"What a good idea!" Mrs. Lloyd said brightly. Maybe they had started Nia on a musical career too early. Perhaps, after all, she had talent. "I'm sure Miss Olwen Oliver wouldn't mind. Nia could sit quietly at the back of the room: It's such a big room, you wouldn't even notice her."

"Well . . ." Catrin's blue eyes widened uncertainly.

"Please?" Nia begged.

Gentle Catrin was persuaded.

Ten minutes later, Nia found herself sitting exactly where she wanted: at the end of Miss Oliver's long chair-lined music room. The chairs were all different sizes and ages, acquired on separate occasions as Miss Oliver's fame and fortune progressed, but very few were comfortable. The faded, floral wallpaper was bare except for black-framed certificates and photographs of successful music students at Eisteddfodau, the local music college. Apart from the two black pianos and the smell of fish, that was it.

The fish smell was a mystery. Miss Oliver was not even a Roman Catholic, and as far as anyone knew, did hardly enough shopping to keep a bird alive. She was a tiny woman, her face a triangle of carved ivory, with a pointed nose and chin, and deep-set black eyes. Her hair, braided and coiled neatly at the nape of her neck, had been white for so long even *she* could barely remember what color it had once been. All these features paled into insignificance behind Miss Olwen Oliver's truly magnificent eyebrows: Long, black, and shaggy, they dominated her every expression, controlled every situation, disciplined every six-foot chorister. No one crossed swords with Miss Oliver's eyebrows, not if they could help it.

Nia had no intention of taking up piano lessons again, the experience had been far too painful.

Miss Oliver had welcomed her in with a rather predatory gleam, and allowed her to choose a chair. "Not too close to the piano, now, or it'll be a distraction for Catrin, who is to take an examination soon, isn't she?"

So Nia chose a chair beside the window, as far from the piano as possible. There was a lace curtain in the window — real lace — a beautiful creamy white, like plum blossoms. The scalloped hem of the curtain hung a good two inches below the window!

Nia took a pair of tiny sewing scissors out of her skirt pocket. Catrin and her teacher were concentrating on Mozart. It was a very beautiful sonata, it reminded Nia of the music Catrin had played at Tŷ Llŷr. Nia had made her dolls dance under the window where the plum trees made green patches on the thick white wall.

Snip! Snip! Snip! She had severed half the hem of the lace curtain. It was all she needed but the other half looked odd now. She cut to the end of the hem, taking her time and carefully following the curves in the lace. How beautifully the patterns parted, how prettily the scalloped hem brushed the windowsill. She'd done Miss Oliver a favor. Nia slipped the strip of deliciously soft lace into her pocket.

Catrin's music lessons always ended with a small display by Miss Oliver, just to show that, whatever level of excellence her pupils had attained, there was still a long way to go before perfection was achieved.

Almost on cue, Catrin's friend Mary McGoohan rang the bell on the last note of Miss Oliver's final flourish.

"Shall I open the door for you?" Nia offered.

"There's a kind girl." Tiny Miss Oliver turned and gave a neat smile. "Perhaps you'd like to take lessons again, Nia?"

"Perhaps." Nia didn't linger. She was out of the music room and opening the front door before Miss Oliver had closed her trim lips.

"I thought you'd given up the piano, Nia," said Mary McGoohan.

"I have!" Nia leaped past her and would have run to number six, but remembering to appear calm, waited for Catrin and walked sedately beside her.

Catrin always sang after her music lesson; her voice was very sweet and soothing. There was no one Nia would rather be with. Catrin was restful and undemanding. One day she would be a star, Nia was sure of that. Catrin was tall and golden, like the girl in a picture on the library wall, painted by a fifteenth-century Italian. Catrin was understanding, she never asked questions. Today, however, she did.

"Are you sleeping better now, Nia?"

"Oh yes!" They had reached number six. "That is, more or less," Nia said cautiously. She opened the black, private door, rushed across the hall, and up the stairs to her room.

Iolo's cars were coming at her in single file across the floor, Iolo behind them, making appropriate revving noises. "Where've you been?" he muttered through the revs.

"Music lesson!" Nia replied. She had expected him to be watching television. Now she couldn't hide the lace in her scrap bags. She stood as close as she could to the chest of drawers, opened the top drawer a fraction, and took the lace from her pocket.

"What're you doing?"

"Getting a hankie," Nia said irritably. She had never known Iolo to be so interested in her movements.

From the bottom of the stairs, Nerys called, "Tea!" and Iolo, always eager to have first choice of whatever was on the table, leaped up and ran out of the room.

Nia tucked the stolen lace under a pile of white socks and followed him.

It was cold roast beef for dinner: Sunday leftovers. Mrs. Lloyd put a slice on Nia's plate. The meat stared up at Nia; it was pink in the middle and Nia found herself saying, "No thanks!"

"What?" Her mother didn't seem to understand.

"I don't want any meat, thank you," Nia said.

"Are you ill, Dear?" Mrs. Lloyd's children had never turned down cold roast beef before.

"No, I'm not ill, I'm a vegetarian!" Nia pushed her plate away.

"What?" Her mother stared at her stupidly, her mouth hanging open like a fish.

"I'm a vegetarian," Nia repeated. *"I don't like meat!"*

The silence that followed reminded her of the time Uncle Maldwyn and Auntie Ann had died, he under his tractor and she an hour later of heart failure. They were nearly eighty but it had still been a shock. Could being a vegetarian be so shocking?

The boys began to giggle, Catrin looked embarrassed, and Nerys had a sort of "I told you so" expression on her face. And then the atmosphere dissolved abruptly as a menacing rumble crescendoed from the end of the table and Mr. Lloyd leaped up roaring, "We'll have no vegetarians here. Meat's my trade!" Here his voice accidentally slipped into a higher register and he had to bang the table to emphasize his words. "Meat! Meat! Meat! Meat!" he squeaked.

Alun's restrained giggle went inward and he snorted piggily. Siôn choked on his orange juice and Iolo laughed out loud.

Nia hunched herself over the table, too close to the pink-tinged slice of meat. She couldn't foresee how it would all end, and then the doorbell rang, hurling her into an even worse situation.

Somehow she knew the identity of their visitor even before her mother opened the front door, and when she heard Miss Olwen Oliver's shrill accusations, her heart sank.

Mrs. Lloyd called Nia into the hall. Her nose was twitching uncontrollably when she left the table and went to face the music.

"Why?"

"Why? Why? Why?" That was all the two women seemed capable of uttering.

And Nia couldn't reply. She couldn't explain why she had severed the beautiful creamy hem of the lace curtain.

The music teacher was in the hall now, her words coming out fast and hysterical. Her tight figure was a tiny rod of pent-up fury. She was literally hopping.

Mr. Lloyd came out of the kitchen, and the boys filled the open doorway behind him. Nerys spread her arms and blocked their passage. Catrin, anxious and bewildered, appeared beside her sister.

Nia backed up toward the stairs. Someone had told her to get the lace. Invisible mending had been mentioned. Punishments were suggested. Abject apologies were made. Nia knew all this, though she scarcely heard the words through the dull ache in her head. And then she remembered something. She stood on the second stair and said, "It was like trees!"

The three adults stared at her.

"What?" said Mr. Lloyd at last. "What did you say, girl?"

"Trees!" Nia repeated in a small voice. "It was like blossoms, you see. And I needed it!"

"Needed it?" Her father was roaring now.

More words, loud and angry, were coming at her like bullets and she fled up to her room. She took the lovely lace from her drawer and brushed it against her cheek. Even now, even when it was the cause of all the wrathful sounds below, she was reluctant to part with it. But she took it downstairs and held it out to Miss Oliver.

"What do you say, girl?" her father muttered.

"I'm sorry," Nia said.

"And are you? Are you?" Miss Oliver's beetle eyebrows closed above her nose.

"Yes!" Nia murmured dutifully and abandoned her parents to a task that was beyond her.

A phrase of her father's rose distinctly above the apologetic noises that she left behind, it was a description of herself. "She's always been a problem, but she seems to be getting worse . . . going up to that chapel . . . cutting up new socks, we think . . ."

Nia closed her bedroom door and went to the window. She watched the sparks in Morgan the Smithy's window. She listened to his sons singing as though there was nothing in the whole wide world to worry about.

She was not sorry for herself, and regretted nothing but the trouble she might have caused Catrin. She had forgotten Catrin when she had cut Miss Oliver's lace, forgotten that poor Catrin would have to face Miss Oliver every week, remembering Nia's crime.

Nia opened her drawer and took out the tiny packet of seeds: honesty, campion, and poppy. She let them roll over her palm while she remembered the garden at Tŷ Llŷr: the brilliance of the poppies and the soft whiteness of the plum trees in spring.

Later, when her mother came into the room, Nia was still sitting on her bed, clasping the seeds.

Mrs. Lloyd sat on Iolo's bed, facing her daughter. She picked up Iolo's woolly blue monster and smoothed its hair. She seemed to be waiting for a word to come from somewhere to bring them closer, but when that did not happen she got up and sat beside Nia on her bed. She was breathing rather fast, and the baby under her dress looked very round and almost unreal. Nia was just wondering if the baby would come soon when her mother asked, "Is it the baby, my love?"

"Baby?" Nia turned to her in surprise.

"Are you worried about us having another baby?"

"Oh no! I'm very pleased. I'm sure I'll like it," Nia said as enthusiastically as she could.

"Is it Tŷ Llŷr then? Would you like to go back?"

"That's impossible."

"No it isn't, actually! We've had an idea. You know how it's spring break next week? Well, Alun's going to stay with Gwyn, and Mrs. Griffiths suggested that you should go, too — and Iolo."

Banished! But what a lucky banishment! "Up to Tŷ Bryn?" Nia could scarcely believe it.

"Would you like that?"

"They don't mind?"

"Of course not. Mrs. Griffiths asked specifically — she wanted to help me out. I'm going to be so busy with Gareth and his leg when he comes home from the hospital."

Alun was a frequent overnight guest at the Griffithses' farmhouse, but Nia had never stayed. She had a sneaking feeling that it was her mother who had begged for a favor, to keep her out of trouble. But she did not care how the situation had come about. She would be going back to the mountain again. She could walk down to Tŷ Llŷr and care for her garden. "What about punishment?" she asked. Surely life could not be so pleasant, not after what she had done.

"No pocket money for a month, your father says! We'll have to pay Mrs. Bowen for invisible mending." Mrs. Lloyd sounded almost apologetic. "And . . . and could you keep from being a vegetarian while you're with the Griffithses? We'll discuss it when you come home."

"There's nothing to discuss. I just am one," Nia said. "But I can be tactful, you know!"

The lace was never mentioned again, and Catrin, such a talented pianist and singer, was never reproached for her sister's crime. Prodigies are sensitive, and Miss Olwen Oliver knew that any deterioration in her favorite pupil's performance would only reflect badly on herself.

CHAPTER SIX
Cold Flowers

MR. GRIFFITHS CAME TO GET ALUN, NIA, AND IOLO THE FOL-
lowing Saturday afternoon.

Iolo wanted to take two toy boxes, but having been persuaded that Gwyn would happily share his possessions, took
only his blue monster.

Nia rolled her canvas in brown paper, and tucked a small bag
of scraps into a suitcase that already contained a muddle of
sweaters, socks, and underwear.

"What've you got there, girl? Not a rolling pin? My wife's
fussy about her pastries!" Mr. Griffiths laughed at his own joke
as no one else seemed inclined to do so.

"It's my work," Nia explained gravely. "Something I have to
do for school."

"I see." Mr. Griffiths was a little disconcerted by Nia's sober
expression. He was aware of her crime, and hoped she wasn't
going to be a problem.

Alun was already in the Land Rover, chatting eagerly to
Gwyn. He glanced resentfully at Nia and Iolo when they
climbed in beside him. He had never had to share Gwyn with

anyone, and he regarded the Griffithses' home as his own, and a refuge from his siblings.

Left-behind-Lloyds spilled out of the door and onto the pavement, waving and shouting instructions as the Land Rover pulled away from the curb, even Gareth with his leg cast and Mr. Lloyd in his striped butcher's apron and funny white hat. Nia wished her father had stayed indoors.

She had to take deep breaths in order to contain her excitement as the Land Rover changed gears and began to ascend the hill out of Pendewi. And then they passed the chapel. She was sitting with her back to it, but she could not resist turning to look into the windows. There was no one there.

Mr. Griffiths drove fast — he resented every minute away from his farm. Gwyn called his father "Demon Driver" and Nia wondered if the name implied talents other than fast driving. He had, after all, fathered a magician.

They were swinging up a familiar lane now. It rose steep and twisting between hedges sprinkled with hawthorn stars and green buds that would soon be honeysuckle. The windows were open, and Nia inhaled the indescribable scent of new growth, of earth disturbed by movement and the sun. Beside the hedge, golden crocuses were opening, and the brook glittered with melting mountain snow. There were crows and curlews tilting in the air, and everywhere the great and mysterious rustling of bright grass reaching toward the sky.

"There's Tŷ Llŷr!" Gwyn said.

"Tŷ Llŷr! Tŷ Llŷr!" shouted Iolo.

And Nia smiled, light-headed now and incapable of speech.

She glimpsed white blossoms, a deserted yard, and two pigeons on a windowsill. Later, she would come and leave a stale crust that Mrs. Griffiths would surely give her.

They passed the white cottage where Gwyn's strange grandmother lived with tall plants in every window and a garden full of herbs. The Land Rover rounded another bend, and then bounced off the lane and up the stone track beside Tŷ Bryn, a farmhouse much neater than Tŷ Llŷr: the porch freshly painted, the path free of weeds, and the flowers beside the stone walls confined in neat pebble-edged borders.

Gwyn's mother was waiting by the front door. She was a shy woman with soft brown hair and eyes to match. She never said much, but she had always been kind. She took Iolo's bundle and would have taken both of Nia's, but Nia clung to her roll of canvas and said she was quite strong enough to carry her suitcase, thank you!

Inside the house everything was clean and tidy, warm and bright. *Wherever we live — us Lloyds — it will never be as neat as this,* Nia thought. And yet, this was where a magician lived.

Gwyn and Alun raced up two flights of stairs to Gwyn's attic room, which they would share.

Nia and Iolo followed Mrs. Griffiths at a more respectful pace, Iolo chewing his monster's arm and looking apprehensive.

They were shown into a room where forget-me-not curtains fluttered in a window and three rag dolls with faded cheeks and button eyes sat on a white dresser. Dolls that looked as though they had been loved once, but now were all forlorn because the person who had loved them had left them.

"It was my Bethan's room, Gwyn's sister, you know," Mrs. Griffiths explained, while Nia stared at the dolls.

Nia was to sleep in a bed covered in bright patchwork, Iolo on a mattress beside the bed.

"Can I go now?" said Iolo, more interested in the outdoors than in bedrooms.

"Of course." Mrs. Griffiths smiled. "I'll unpack your things, Iolo. Let's put your monster on the bed, all right? There are white rabbits in the orchard."

"Aww!" Iolo rushed out. He wouldn't leave his monster, though.

"Are they wild?" Nia asked.

"Wild?" Mrs. Griffiths looked confused.

"The rabbits!"

"Oh no!" Mrs. Griffiths laughed. "They're in a hutch. We couldn't have them out eating our lettuce, could we?"

"I suppose not," Nia said solemnly. "I'll unpack Iolo's things. I'd like to."

"Well, if you want to." Mrs. Griffiths hesitated. "I'll go back to my cooking. I'm not used to cooking for so many. I hope I get it right."

"I bet you will," Nia said with a smile she had been told was the best part of her.

Quite unexpectedly, Mrs. Griffiths put her arms around Nia and hugged her quickly. "It's good to have a girl in the house," she said.

Nia, taken by surprise, murmured, "I'll try . . ." but did not know how to finish the sentence, and said instead, "Could I go down to Tŷ Llŷr and see my garden?"

"Well, of course, Dear." Mrs. Griffiths, a neat, aproned housewife again, rushed out. "And visit Gwyn's Nain," she called from the stairs. "She'll be pleased to see you."

Gwyn's grandmother doesn't know me, Nia thought. "And I'm not going into that place alone," she said to the rag dolls.

The dolls looked sympathetic. They watched Nia unpack her bag and open a drawer in the dresser. A dry sweet smell wafted out: *roses*! Nia opened the closet. There were clothes inside — another girl's clothes: a yellow skirt, a gray coat, and a blue dress with flowers on it. She began to remember someone: a girl with dark hair and eyes very like herself, a girl in a blue dress picking flowers in the lane. The closet smelled of roses, too.

Bethan's room softly enclosed her, settled smoothly and easily around her, as though she fitted exactly into a space in the dust that had been occupied only a moment before by someone else.

Nia unpacked Iolo's bag and began to lay his clothes in the second drawer, but seeing her reflection in the mirror, paused to loosen her long braids of dark hair. The girl who now looked out at her belonged in a room with forget-me-not curtains and the scent of roses. The rag dolls smiled with approval.

She closed the drawer, took one happy look around the room that was to be hers for a week, and went downstairs.

The boys were in the orchard, gathered around a pen where two white rabbits leaped enthusiastically about in a pile of fresh dandelion leaves.

Fly bounded out of nowhere, greeting Nia with a display of delighted barking and rolling.

"I'm going to Tŷ Llŷr," Nia called. She was glad no one responded. She wanted the place to herself. Fly was keen to accompany her, though. "Stay," said Nia, rather too severely. "You're Gwyn's dog now."

She ran all the way, only slowing her pace when she passed Gwyn's grandmother in her garden. The old woman was leaning on a hoe, peering at a patch of earth.

"*Bore da,*" said Nia, knowing that the older Mrs. Griffiths preferred to hear Welsh.

Mrs. Griffiths looked up, her thoughts still with the patch of earth or whatever it was that should or should not be growing there. She wore a big straw hat squashed down over black curls. Her eyes could not be seen.

Receiving no reply to what she had considered a polite greeting, Nia ran on to Tŷ Llŷr. She didn't linger in the yard where the ghosts of hens gathered into awful emptiness. She didn't peep into the windows where rooms that she had known would be slowly dying. She ran straight to her wild garden by the stream — and received a great surprise.

Someone had been there. The earth around her poppies was brown and freshly turned, there were no weeds to strangle the orange-gold flowers. And how they had flourished! Divided and replanted, they covered the ground in huge brilliant clusters.

"Oh!" Nia cried. "Who did it?"

Beyond the poppies where thick rushes crept up the bank, someone had built a low stone wall, three layers deep, to keep the weeds at bay, and here and there blue forget-me-nots grew, like tiny pieces of reflected sky.

There was nothing for Nia to do but sit beside her flowers and watch the water.

"I'll forget the church and those old evergreens," she muttered, thinking of her canvas, "and I'll make Tŷ Llŷr and my garden." She wondered if she could persuade Mrs. Griffiths to find some yellow cloth. She had a feeling she would be offered a dust rag.

Happier now and confident, she walked back to the house and risked a quick peek in her old home. She chose a window overhung with the blossoms of two ancient plum trees that curved toward each other from either side. Ghosts of absent furniture stood against the walls; pale shapes on the stained and lived-in wallpaper: a cupboard, a dresser, a silent piano. The only three-dimensional furnishing now was a neat pile of torn paper in a corner. A home for a mouse!

As she stepped away from the window she almost stepped on the soldier: a small knit soldier with a red coat, a stripe of yellow buttons, and a tall black hat. Not a Lloyd toy — she knew every one of those. Nia slipped the soldier into her pocket.

Two pigeons, were pecking in the yard. If Mr. Butcher Lloyd had been there, he would have run for his gun. "Pigeons are pests," he would say. "They'll eat my seeds." If Mr. Lloyd had been there, the pigeons would have left. But this year they would nest in the sycamore tree, and there might be four or five pigeons living at Tŷ Llŷr. Nia wished she had remembered to bring bread crusts.

She wandered out of the yard, closing the big gate out of habit, though now there was no reason to do so.

Nain Griffiths was standing by her garden wall when Nia passed, as though she had been waiting. She was wearing a purple cardigan so bright it was almost shouting, and there were pearly pink parrots swinging from her ears.

"Hello!" said Nia, over the wall.

"*Bore da Nia,*" returned Gwyn's grandmother.

"You know my name?" said Nia, astonished.

"I know my neighbors, don't I?" said old Mrs. Griffiths.

"But you knew which one I was — you knew I was Nia. Nobody ever knows me because I'm in the middle!"

"Well, I know you, don't I?" The dark and wrinkled face came closer, pink birds quivering under gray-black curls. "I don't know any of the others, but I know you!"

"Oh!" Nia stepped back, but not to be outdone she asked, "Have you been weeding my garden?"

"Weeding?"

"Yes. I've got poppies by the stream and someone has been caring for them, doing some gardening there. Was it you?"

"Don't you think I've got enough to do?" Gwyn's grandmother heaved a forkful of stringy weeds above the gate. A shower of mud and leaves flew into the air, some landing on Nia's head.

"Sorry!" said Nia. "It was just a guess." It was not she who should have apologized, she thought, but it was quite evident that old Mrs. Griffiths did not regret showering her with mud. Nia began to run up the lane.

"*Pob hwyl!*" Nain Griffiths called after her. "Come and see me soon."

"Same to you!" Nia shouted without turning. She didn't think she would call on Gwyn's grandmother again if she could help it.

After a lunch of shepherd's pie that was much better than Nia had expected, the boys announced that they were going to walk up the mountain.

"And what about Nia?" Mr. Griffiths could have been smiling under his heavy mustache. It was difficult to tell.

"I might, that is I . . ." Nia hesitated.

"Going to help clean up the henhouse after, are you, then?"

"Well . . ." Nia began. "Someone's been in the garden at Tŷ Llŷr," she said, changing the subject. "Caring for my plants, building a little wall . . ."

Mr. Griffiths gaped speechlessly at Nia. It was as if she had said there were wolves in the woods.

Mrs. Griffiths was doing the dishes. She didn't see her husband's face. "I'm afraid I don't have time for other people's gardens," she said. "Perhaps it was Nain."

"No," said Nia. "I asked her." She was fascinated by Mr. Griffiths's discomfort.

Shifting away from Nia's disturbing scrutiny, Mr. Griffiths left the kitchen without a word and went out into the yard.

"Perhaps it was Gwyn," Nia persisted.

"Gwyn's no gardener," Mrs. Griffiths replied. "His sister was, though!" She suddenly dropped a pan and became quite still, her shoulders hunched and her hands motionless in the soapy water. Nia couldn't see her expression, but her voice changed pitch and she said, "Why don't you run along now and follow the boys?"

Nia went. Why had her garden caused such a stir?

The boys were wandering up the mountain track, surrounded by ewes and their fat, excitable lambs. The air was full of noisy bleating. Iolo was happily echoing the sounds; he'd abandoned his woolly monster at last.

Nia did not catch up with the boys, she did not intend to. They passed the stone wall where the track rose away from the field and disappeared from sight.

Nia left the track and walked on through the field. She could hear the boys above her, climbing now and shouting to one another.

Nia was in the Griffithses' land, but she knew it well. The mountain had belonged to her mother's family, the Llŷrs, and their sheep, for as long as anyone could remember. Her feet fitted well into the hard, slanting land. She wandered south, toward the sun, while the voices above her became lost in the chorus of sheep and streams.

She had been walking for a mile up and down, still in the same landscape, when she came upon a place she could not remember: a valley lay below her, where blossoms floated like clouds among darker trees. An orchard of palest pink apple blossoms swept like a crescent moon around a low cottage with a mossy green roof and smoke drifting from the chimney. Perhaps she had never been there in the spring, never looked down into the valley. It was the blossoms that had made her look.

Nia began to walk down into the trees. The ground became steeper, and she was suddenly hurled into a rushing, sliding descent. Breathless and frightened, she caught hold of a branch and saw a path, narrow but well trodden, that wound between the trees. Someone often came this way. But there was no place for a car or a vehicle of any kind.

On the path, her pace became more dignified. She had time to observe the land before her. The woods were ancient: oak and ash trees, their branches dappled with the pale green of leaves not fully grown; delicate rowan and bushy hazel, and now and then a holly tree, shining dark and dangerous in the distance. And then Nia was in the orchard. The sun was high, sparkling through the bright canopy of blossoms. But Nia was cold! She was walking through flowers — tall and dense, they covered the ground beneath the apple trees. They were white flowers, huge blooms, like stars on tall stems, their leaves broad spears of emerald.

Nia bent to pick a flower and gasped: It was like touching ice!

CHAPTER SEVEN
A Visit to Nain Griffiths

HOLDING THE FLOWER CAUTIOUSLY BY THE STEM, NIA MOVED through the orchard. The cold began to penetrate her shoes and socks, it moved up her body and she began to shiver. She might have been walking through a field of snow.

She emerged from the orchard and came into a garden where the low cottage stood surrounded by wildflowers. It seemed to be utterly deserted. Lost. The silence was profound. Yet smoke still drifted from the chimney.

All at once Nia became aware that she was trespassing, that this was a very secret and private place. She turned back into the orchard and began to run. She ran from the silence and the cold white flowers.

Stumbling over brambles and loose rocks that seemed, suddenly, to have invaded the well-trodden path, Nia began to make her way out of the valley. The valley, it appeared, was reluctant to let her go. It tried to halt her progress with stones that slid beneath her feet, with wet and slippery stalks, twigs that got caught in her loose hair, and thorns that scratched her face. She threaded the white flower into her hair, freeing her hands to protect her face. The ground was surely steeper than it had been on her descent. Nia began to panic. She could see a misty rim of trees at the top of the valley, and climbed toward them, but in doing so lost the path. The quiet woods closed in upon her, a damp blanket of decaying leaves smothered her feet, and tired and uncertain, she stopped moving. "Nerys would say a poem," she muttered aloud. "Catrin would sing! But Nia Can't Do Nothing. Nia is trapped!"

"Nia *can* do something!" admonished Idris Llewelyn, who had assumed the shape of a broad oak.

Pulling her feet through the leaves, Nia ran toward a bank and climbed upward, hand over hand, until she burst through bushes of sweet-smelling elderflowers, and fell into a field where sheep stared anxiously at her sudden and violent arrival.

"All right, so I was scared," Nia said to her audience, "but I didn't notice any of *you* down there!"

The sheep regarded her, unblinking. A few spoke back, and then they frightened themselves into a wild and disorganized retreat.

"Who's scared now?" Nia called after them and laughed. She felt safe out in the rough sunlit field, and ran happily all the way back to the farmhouse.

The boys were already there. Their muddy boots were on the porch.

"They're up in Gwyn's room!" Mrs. Griffiths told Nia.

She climbed the stairs quickly, reluctant to intrude on male territory, but eager to discuss her adventure.

"Where've you been?" Alun asked suspiciously when Nia walked in on them. "We called and called!"

"Just walking," she replied. "I haven't done anything that I shouldn't have!"

Alun looked relieved. "Gwyn's rabbits are expecting," he said. "We can have some of the babies and keep them in a hutch out in the yard at number six."

"Dad would kill them!" The words spilled out — she still resented Alun's first question.

The boys looked appalled.

"He would never . . ." Alun said at last.

"He would!" Nia couldn't stop herself. "It's his trade now. He'd chop off their heads and hang them in his window."

"You're mean, Nia," Iolo cried. "Our dad would never kill white rabbits. They'd be ours — our pets!"

"What's that?" Gwyn was staring at the white flower hanging in Nia's hair. She had forgotten it.

"I found it in a valley," she said. "A valley I never noticed before, with an orchard and a stone cottage."

Gwyn came over and took the flower out of her hair. No one but Nia heard his quiet gasp as he touched it. "It's cold," he said.

"And it shines," Alun remarked. "It's like those luminous stars on your watch, Gwyn."

Gwyn cupped his hands around the starlike petals. He gazed at the flower, saying nothing. The others looked down into the dark cradle of Gwyn's hands. Each petal glowed like a Christmas light.

"Awww!" Iolo exclaimed. "It's beeee-yooteeful!"

"There are lots of them in the valley," Nia said. "Thousands. Can I have it now?"

Gwyn held the flower out to her. "There are some in our garden, too," he said thoughtfully. "But they're not so big and they don't shine. My sister planted them."

Mrs. Griffiths called them to dinner and they tumbled out of Gwyn's attic room, down the twelve ladder steps that led to it, across the narrow landing, and then down the conventional and carpeted staircase. The mountain air had made them hungry.

They crowded expectantly around the long kitchen table where plates of fruitcake and sandwiches had been laid on a white cloth.

"May I have a glass?" Nia asked Mrs. Griffiths. "It's for my flower. Look!"

"Well, well, I never! It's beautiful, Nia. Where did you find it?"

"In a valley," Nia replied, "with an orchard and a little cottage. There were hundreds of them."

Mr. Griffiths, already drinking tea at the table, looked up. "I wouldn't go there, girl!" he said sternly.

"Why not?" Nia couldn't stop herself.

"Because I say not to, that's why!" Gwyn's father barked out.

The children, subdued, sat down and began to eat their dinner.

Mrs. Griffiths put Nia's flower in a tall glass and placed it on the table, but after the meal Nia took it up to her room and set it on the dresser beside the rag dolls. They brightened in its presence, as though the dust of four years had been swept off their raggedy faces and pretty cotton clothes.

The Griffiths family went to bed early. Nia lay in her new room listening to Gwyn's parents moving around on the other side of the hall. She heard Gwyn and Alun murmuring in their attic. Iolo fell asleep on his mattress beside her bed.

Nia couldn't close her eyes. The pale flower glowed in the dark, its reflection in the mirror sending points of light dancing into the room. Why were so many places forbidden? First the Llewelyns' chapel, now the orchard valley, and it all came back to solitary, gloomy Mr. Griffiths.

Wide awake, she crept to the window and drew back the forget-me-not curtains. The round shadow of the earth almost obliterated the moon; only a tiny sliver was left, hanging like a sickle among the myriad distant stars.

Nia turned on her bedside light. Undisturbed, Iolo slept soundly in shadow on the other side of her bed. She took her canvas from a rose-scented drawer and rolled it out. One corner insisted on curling upward so she set the rag dolls on the offending place and spread glue across the top of the canvas. She took a length of dark blue velvet from her rag bag, cut it into a shape, and pressed it onto the glue. A midnight sky! She dotted the velvet with glue and shook glitter onto the dots. The glitter clustered in bright constellations, just as she wanted. Bethan's dolls looked on with interest.

Nia worked well. She cut green for the grass; violet, black, and brown for the trees and their shadows; gray for the stone walls; purple for foxgloves and yellow for buttercups, but there was nothing in her bag that would work for her special orange-gold poppies.

When she turned off her light and climbed into bed, the multicolored rooster was crowing from his perch.

Nia tackled the problem of the poppies after breakfast the next morning. Mrs. Griffiths was kneading dough on the kitchen table.

"Have you got a piece of cloth, orangey-gold, like the poppies at Tŷ Llŷr?"

"What for, Dear?"

"My work," Nia replied. She felt it was unnecessary to give any more information.

"I see," Mrs. Griffiths seemed to find Nia's answer adequate. She rinsed her floury fingers under the faucet, and went to a cupboard.

"There's all kinds of cloth in here." She pulled out a large box and set it on the kitchen table. The box was stuffed with pieces of torn shirts, holey socks, and even underwear. Mrs. Griffiths held up a faded T-shirt.

Nia shook her head. "It has to be like the poppies."

"Well, that's all there is. You could dye something, I suppose. Go and see Gwyn's grandmother — she knows all about dye, she does it with flowers and herbs."

"No. I don't want to go there, thanks!"

"Why not?" Mrs. Griffiths seemed disconcerted by Nia's candor.

"She's peculiar. And I don't fancy going in that dark old place with all those plants poking at me."

Mrs. Griffiths laughed. "What a strange girl you are, Nia Lloyd!" She went to the door and called, "Gwyn, come here. I want you to take Nia down to see Nain."

Gwyn came rattling down the stairs. Alun and Iolo followed, less enthusiastically.

"What's going on?" Gwyn asked.

Mrs. Griffiths put the T-shirt into Nia's hands. "Nia has to dye something. Nain will show her how."

"Aw, come on," moaned Alun. "We don't have to go, do we?"

"I don't want to," Iolo added nervously, from behind his brother.

"There'd be no room in there for you two, anyway," Gwyn assured him. "We won't be long." He was about to rush out the front door when he suddenly stopped and said to Nia, "Bring the flower!"

Grateful, Nia ran up to the bedroom and took the white flower out of the glass. Was it her imagination or had the flower grown in the night? She took it downstairs and gave it to Gwyn. He frowned at it, puzzled, and then said, "Come on!"

They left Alun and Iolo in the lane, playing with Fly. The young sheepdog seemed to have forgotten her nightmare at number six. Her barks were joyful here. Nia thought of Emlyn.

But Gwyn had other things on his mind. He was staring at the flower, gingerly touching the icy petals with his forefinger.

They walked in silence until they reached a white gate with the name COED MELYN — The Yellow Wood — painted in green upon it.

Nia stopped, twisting the T-shirt in her hands.

"She won't bite!" Gwyn grinned.

"Won't she?" Nia followed Gwyn through the gate and up a gravel path bordered with tall, fragrant flowers. The door was opened before they had reached it, and Gwyn's grandmother stood on her step, dressed all in red, with a gold belt around her waist and rings on every finger.

"Has your prince come then, Nain?" Gwyn asked his grandmother.

"Not yet! Not yet!" The old woman giggled at their private joke. "Who's this, then?" She poked a finger at Nia.

"You know who I am!" Nia said fiercely. "You said you knew."

"Just testing!" Nain Griffiths laid her ringed fingers on Nia's arm and drew her into the room beyond.

It was not as bad as Nia expected. Dark, yes, but colorful, and the plants that lived there jostled with ropes of beads, painted pottery, ancient jeweled boxes, ostrich feathers, and exotic shawls. You could hardly see the furniture beneath. Such splendors could not be appreciated by a quick peek through a window, and that was all that Nia had ventured until today.

"Take a seat and I'll bring you rose-hip syrup," Nain commanded and disappeared behind a screen.

The only seats were patchwork cushions on the floor. A black hen slept in the armchair. The children sat down, and Nia found she had settled beside a white cat in a glass box. Her nose began its nervous twitching.

Nain Griffiths reappeared and gave the children mugs of warm rosy liquid. Nia sipped suspiciously, but it was very good.

"Look at this, Nain," Gwyn said, offering her the white flower. "Feel the petals!"

Nain Griffiths took the flower. She sniffed it, touched it, gasped, and regarded it with her head to one side, as though listening for a message from the ground. "Well, I don't know," she murmured. "It's not of this earth, child. It doesn't belong here!" and she darted a look at Gwyn, so fierce and full of meaning that Nia was quite shaken.

"What is it?" she asked.

Gwyn and his grandmother looked at her, and then Gwyn said, "Two years ago my sister came back. I called her with . . ." He hesitated, looked at his hands, and then at his grandmother who nodded approvingly. ". . . with the power I inherited from my ancestors."

"Back from the dead?" Nia whispered.

"She's not dead!" Gwyn's black eyes were fathomless. "She's out there." He looked toward the chinks of sky behind the red flowers in the window. Somehow Nia knew that he meant to indicate a place beyond the sky. "They took her," he went on. "Things that look like children but aren't human. Icy things that smile and sing and make you want to be with them. Bethan wanted to go, and they took her. She's happy there, she said."

"Where?" Nia's throat was dry, and the question came out in a frightened croak.

"On a planet of ice, where everything is covered in snow. She'd changed her name and she was cold and pale, even the color of her eyes had been washed away."

"How did you call her?" Nia found a small tight voice. Gwyn seemed to have brought frost into the room.

"I had her scarf" — he smiled slyly, the way a wizard might — "and I gave it to the wind. Do you know about Gwydion the magician, and the seaweed?"

"He made a ship," she said, and because she almost knew what Gwyn was going to tell her, added, "out of seaweed."

"Gwydion lived in these mountains," Gwyn said. "Sometimes I think he's still here inside me." He looked at his fingers: long, sinewy fingers, too long for a boy. "Nain gave me seaweed for my birthday." He glanced at his grandmother, tall and crimson, her eyes fixed on her grandson, reliving with him the moment when the strange inherited power had awakened in him. "I threw my seaweed from the mountain, and a ship fell out of space. It was silver and there were icicles clinging to it. The cold of it hurt my eyes, hurt all of me, and I could barely see. It brought my sister back."

Nia stared at Gwyn and at his young-old hands. She had seen his power in the churchyard. "Where is Bethan now?" she asked softly.

"She went back."

"How?"

"On the ship. Alun knows."

"Alun?" How had Alun managed to keep a secret like that? And then Nia remembered the time he had been lost in snow on the mountain but had miraculously survived. Gwyn had saved him somehow with the power that no one believed in.

"At school they teased you," she said.

"Children are cruel," Nain muttered, "when they don't believe."

Nia had no such difficulty. "It was very cold the day we moved from Tŷ Llŷr," she went on. "It came suddenly. Was it the ship? Did you call your sister again?"

"No. I didn't call. There's something I don't understand," said Gwyn. "Perhaps it has to do with the flower."

Nain brought the flower close to her face. Shadows appeared on her strange, lined features. She was beautiful, Nia realized, in a way that rocks and trees and ancient polished things were beautiful.

They sipped their sweet drink for a while, and then Nia said, "You used your power on Emlyn Llewelyn."

"What?" said Nain Griffiths. "What's this I hear, Gwydion Gwyn? Did you abuse your power?"

"No, Nain," Gwyn cried. "I never hurt him. I had to stop him for a while. He was angry, unreasonable." And he told Nain about Nia and Fly, about the dog's leash and the fight in the churchyard. "But I let him win, Nain," he finished. "I knew I had to do that!"

"That may be," said Nain, "but it's not right what your father and the town have done to Emlyn Llewelyn."

Nia had never heard anyone state Emlyn's point of view. "Why?" she asked.

"They're ignorant," Nain said scathingly. "Idris Llewelyn is an artist, trying to do his best, making things beautiful. And there is his wife, Gwyn's aunt, leaving her husband and her own boy just because she hasn't got electricity!"

Gwyn jumped up. "She couldn't live in that old chapel. She wanted a proper home for her baby. Uncle Idris was cruel and wicked, Dad says."

"Emlyn stayed," Nia said quietly.

"He should have gone with his mom, he should have!" Gwyn retorted.

"Emlyn stayed because he knows what's right. He's loyal and he's brave, and you and he should be friends, Gwydion Gwyn, and not fighting in a sacred place, where you know the power is all on your side!" Nain's tone was not unkind, but Gwyn turned from her resentfully as she passed him and whisked the T-shirt out of Nia's hands. "Now let us see what we can do with this!" she said.

"How did you know?" asked Nia, astonished.

"I can't imagine you would visit me just for pleasure, Nia Lloyd," Nain teased.

Nia did not answer that statement. "I wanted to make some orange cloth," she confessed. "It's for my work. I want to make it the color of Welsh poppies — my own special poppies by the stream at Tŷ Llŷr. Gwyn's mom said you could do it."

Nain beckoned Nia from behind the yellow screen into her kitchen. Nia followed cautiously. She watched Nain Griffiths take a large enamel pot from the wall, fill it with water, and set it on her stove. "First, onion skins," Nain muttered and pulled six onions from a neatly braided string hanging from the low-beamed ceiling. "Peel them!" she commanded, handing Nia the onions.

Nia put them on the table and began to dig her nails into the crackling skins. Her eyes stung and as she looked up to wipe the tears away, she heard the front door bang and Gwyn's footsteps running up the lane.

"Don't cry," Nain Griffiths chuckled. "He's a sensitive boy but he'll come around. And you needn't be afraid of me!"

"It's the onions," said Nia, annoyed by the tears. "And I'm not afraid."

The hours that then sped by seemed more like five minutes. Nia stood by while Gwyn's grandmother stirred a boiling liquid of onion skins and lichen until it turned golden. Into this bubbling, syrupy water she dropped the faded T-shirt which had first been washed by Nia in the sink. They then took turns with the stirring, using a wooden spoon as long as Nia's arm, and while they stirred, Nain told Nia about the boy who had just left them. About the line of magic that stretched back through her family to a time when princes and magicians ruled Wales, and the people that Nia had thought were only part of a story became as real to her as the mountain beyond Nain's door. She saw a time and place where enchantment was a necessity, the lifeblood of an ancient people, who had changed and grown through invasion and suppression, still keeping a small piece of magic inside themselves until, once every century perhaps, it bubbled out and a magician was driven to secrecy, like Gwyn Griffiths.

"And you have it, too, Nia Lloyd!" said Nain, breaking into Nia's thoughts.

"Me?" she exclaimed, amazed. "But I'm no one. I'm in the middle. I Can't Do Nothing!"

"What's this, then?" Nain lifted a spoonful of golden liquid and let it trickle back into the pot. "Turning white cloth to gold, isn't it? And aren't you a Llŷr, whose ancestors once ruled Britain? There's a little bit of power left inside you, Nia Lloyd, if you look for it!"

The shirt was pulled out and hung, steaming from the huge spoon, darker by several shades. It was thrust under cold water, squeezed and put on the stove to dry, while Nain and Nia nibbled cookies made of oats and berries.

"You'll have to leave the cloth with me for a day or two, for the dye to set," Nain told Nia. "But you'll come again, won't you, if you need more colors?"

"Oh I will," Nia replied fervently.

When she left Coed Melyn she was older by far more than a few hours. And she was stronger, strong enough, perhaps, to bring together two boys who had been divided by a silly quarrel that had nothing to do with them.

CHAPTER EIGHT

The Wrong Reflection

NIA KEPT TO HERSELF FOR THE REST OF SPRING BREAK. SHE did not mention Emlyn again. The days were warm and dry; days for the boys to help with fence-mending, stone-wall-building, and sheep-shearing, and for playing barefoot in the streams when their work was done.

Nia was excused from farm duties and allowed to work in Bethan's room. Through the open window the boys' cheerful voices were companionable and undemanding. She worked well. The canvas began to come to life.

Nain Griffiths came to the house one day, holding a piece of bright cloth, as gloriously golden-orange as a bouquet of poppies. And that night Nia cut her poppies into their proper shapes and sewed them neatly in place beside a stream of silver tinsel and blue forget-me-nots that had once been Mrs. Bowen's satin underwear.

By the end of the week, Nia had recovered her confidence sufficiently to believe that she could, after all, visit the Llewelyns again. She would say she had come to get the violet dress and

Mr. Llewelyn would welcome her in and finish her portrait. Emlyn would have to forgive her.

Happily absorbed in future plans, Nia left Tŷ Bryn believing that her canvas could be a masterpiece, and that her friendship with Emlyn would surely be renewed.

As she said good-bye to Mrs. Griffiths, she told her, "It's the best vacation I ever had, anywhere!" And she meant it.

Mrs. Griffiths seemed sad at their departure. "We don't see enough girls up here," she said wistfully. "Come again, Dear!"

"If you'll have me." Nia beamed.

Gwyn was nowhere to be seen. She hoped he didn't regret the secrets he had told her.

Nain Griffiths was standing by her gate when the Land Rover bounced past. She was wearing a dress she had dipped in the bowl of Nia's poppy-gold dye. She did a little dance and blew a kiss. Nia had to laugh. She knelt on the seat and leaned out of the window. "You're a poppy!" she cried, and waved until the bright figure was out of sight.

"Gwyn's grandmother is crazy!" Alun remarked.

"She's not! She's fantastic!" Nia leaped down and glared at Alun. "I think she's a great lady, would have been a queen, probably, if the Anglo-Saxons hadn't come, and all those others!"

All at once, Mr. Griffiths began to roar with laughter. He couldn't stop. It was such an unusual sound coming from him; the children stared at his shaking back in perplexity, and Alun couldn't decide who was the craziest, his sister or his best friend's family.

Number six seemed unbearably dark and gloomy after the clear mountain light. There were sheets and shirts mounded on chairs, waiting to be ironed. Stained butcher's aprons were piled by the washing machine. Gareth, with his autographed white leg cast, was somehow everywhere, moaning because he "couldn't sit down nowhere!" He'd tried putting his foot on a chair and smashed a lens in Nerys's spectacles.

Nerys was in a horrendous mood. Her new hairdo had gone wrong: Mousy spikes framed her long face, and she regarded everything with a slit-eyed furious glance. Siôn was fed up with Gareth's moaning and even calm Catrin was thumping out Mozart like she was tackling a football player.

Nia had brought her white flower, the stem wrapped carefully in damp tissue. To save bothering her mother she put the flower in her blue toothbrush holder and set it on the windowsill. It looked as bright and as fresh as ever.

Mrs. Lloyd had forgotten that she would have three extra for tea, and it was Sunday, so she couldn't run to the store.

"I don't need cake," Nia informed them. "I want to go and see Gwyneth. I've got to ask her something about school. Can I go now?"

"Well, if it's about school . . ." Mrs. Lloyd gratefully cut the remaining piece of fruitcake into eight neat slices.

Nia squeezed between the dresser and her brothers on their bench, happily relinquishing fruitcake in order to escape.

"Won't be long!" she called confidently from the hall.

Outside she did not feel so sure of herself. The walk up to the chapel seemed longer than usual, but she did not have to knock.

Idris Llewelyn was painting silver leaves beneath the gold flowers on his door. "I hadn't finished," he told Nia, "but it's done now. Do you approve?"

Nia nodded and followed him into the chapel. Emlyn was sitting on the floor with a book. He did not look at her.

"Well, get up, boy, and welcome your visitor," said Mr. Llewelyn. He prodded his son gently with a sandaled foot. "I heard about the fight he had with you and his cousin about the dog."

"It wasn't my fault," Nia blurted out. "Dad sold it to Mr. Griffiths. I tried to stop him. But I couldn't . . . couldn't tell you. I was a coward!"

"Not a coward, just cautious. And Emlyn is sorry! Aren't you, boy? He went to see you during school break."

"Did you?" Nia looked at Emlyn in surprise. She perched herself on a cushion beside him, but he still refused to respond. *He hasn't forgiven me — he never will,* she thought.

"You weren't there," he said at last, still without looking at her. "That sister of yours opened the door. The one with glasses. I'm sorry, but I can't stand her."

"I know what you mean," Nia said. Now and again there were good reasons for being disloyal. "Did she say something spiteful? They didn't want me to come here again. They sent me away, up to Gwyn Griffiths's place, with Alun and Iolo. I'd gotten in trouble, see!"

"Trouble?" Mr. Llewelyn sounded concerned.

"I thought everyone would know by now. Miss Olwen Oliver is famous gossiping."

"We haven't seen anyone," Emlyn murmured. "No one comes here."

"Tell us your trouble, girl." Mr. Llewelyn put his silvery brush into a jar and sat on an extraordinarily large, upturned bucket.

"The first thing was," Nia began, "I said I was a vegetarian."

Emlyn looked up.

"Well, that didn't go down too well, Dad being a butcher and all. The next thing happened because I wanted something for blossoms and I couldn't think what, so I . . . so I . . ."

"Go on," Emlyn said with a spark of interest.

"So I cut a piece of lace from Miss Olwen Oliver's curtain. I did that before saying I was a vegetarian, but they didn't know," Nia said in a rush. "I didn't think it would be noticeable. And wow, there was so much trouble." She sighed and rolled her eyes toward the ceiling, remembering the horror of it all.

When she dared to observe the effect her confession had made, she found that Mr. Llewelyn's very white teeth were showing through the mass of brown hair on his face. He was smiling, and then he was laughing, and Emlyn with him.

"But it was a terrible thing I did," Nia reproached them.

"It was! It was!" agreed Mr. Llewelyn. "Excuse us! Why didn't you come to us? We can give you lace and anything you need for your masterpiece." He strode to a wooden box beneath one of the long windows and flung it open. "Look!" He exclaimed. "Lace and cotton, feathers and pretty things!" He held up a dress, the palest of pink cotton embossed with white flowers. "Blossoms! Don't you agree?"

The children stood simultaneously. Emlyn was staring at his father and at the dress.

"What do you think, Emlyn? Shall I give this to Nia for her work?" His words were somehow more than a question.

Emlyn was still gazing at the dress. He screwed up his face, like someone with toothache. "I don't mind," he said at last.

"No coat to hide it in today," observed Mr. Llewelyn. "Will you dare to say you got the dress from us?"

"I'll say it was from Gwyneth Bowen. I'm always getting wool and stuff out of her mom's shop. They'll believe me."

"Nia Lloyd, you have criminal tendencies," Idris Llewelyn remarked with half a smile.

"No, I never . . ." she began, but the big man laughed again and bundled the dress into her arms.

"Will you stay for tea?" he asked.

Nia hesitated. She dared not risk getting into trouble on her first day at home. "I'll come tomorrow," she said.

When she left, Emlyn followed her out onto the road, but no farther. He sat on the chapel steps and when she turned back to wave he would not look at her; his chin was cupped in his hands and he was staring out at distant, empty mountains.

He hasn't forgiven me, Nia thought. *But he will, he must!*

Everything at number six had simmered down, by the time Nia returned. The boys were by the river examining something dead on the bank. The river was low and so was the sun. The water sparkled gold over smooth stones and bare feet.

"What's that?" Iolo poked a wet finger at the dress in Nia's arms.

"Don't!" she sprang back. "It's for my work."

"Oh!" He fished a handkerchief from his pocket and a match-box came tumbling out and fell into a shallow pool at his feet. "Aw, no!" he cried, retrieving the damp box. "Nia, take it inside for me, will you?"

"What is it?"

"A spider! I found it at Gwyn's place. It's special, like silver!"

Nia took the box and left them to decide the identity of the dead fish. She passed the window of her father's cold room. She told herself not to look in, but did. The sight was even more gory than she had imagined. Her father was removing unimaginable things from something lying on a bloody slab — and he was whistling!

She ran up to her room where curiosity prompted her to open Iolo's matchbox. The spider was, indeed, special: very tiny, silvery, and like the white flower, it seemed to glow.

She put the box on the chest of drawers, slightly open so that the spider could breathe or spin, or do anything a spider should do.

The boys would be in the river for hours, she could tell. There was no one to bother her. She knelt down and spread the dress on the floor. It was almost too beautiful to cut, but someone had already done that. The hem had been unevenly severed — slashed hastily as though with a knife.

The sight was somehow rather shocking. Nia scissored away the painful gashes, neatening the wound, tidying the sad, pale dress. She put the severed strands into a rag bag and then, almost by accident, found herself slipping the dress over her head. The cuffs of the long, full sleeves covered her fingers, and the high collar tickled her neck very softly.

She smoothed the dress close to her body, over her skirt and crumpled shirt. It concealed everything but her sneakers. Elinor Llewelyn must have been tall and slim.

Nia wished she could see herself. A mirror had been promised once. In their room, Catrin and Nerys had a mirror that reached to the floor, but Nerys was probably there reading.

Sometimes a hint of a reflection would emerge from the wardrobe's shiny doors. Today, to Nia's amazement, there was more than a hint. A huge circle of shimmering silver hung over the doors: a cobweb spun so fine, so close, it resembled a mirror. How it had come there and when, Nia could not imagine, but it must have been the work of Iolo's spider because there it was, at the very top, swinging on an inch of gossamer.

The window was open and the web was blown into a slow, deep movement, like a wave. Nia waited for it to calm. She could already see the pink dress and dark hair above it, like someone lying under clear water. Gradually features began to appear: large dark eyes, a pale face and lips, parted in a scream. The face that looked out at Nia was not hers.

Nia screamed, and went on screaming. She gasped for air, terrified and trembling.

"Nia, what is it?" Catrin stood behind her, clasping her shoulders.

"Not me! It's not me!" sobbed Nia. "Not my face!" She pointed to where a dark woman's features had replaced her own, but the shining cobweb had broken loose. A cloud of silvery threads streamed toward them and drifted out through the open window.

CHAPTER NINE
Children After Midnight

LATER, WHEN NIA HAD RECOVERED AND MOM SAT READING BY her bed, the spider crawled over the carved pattern at the top of the closet. The tiny creature mesmerized her, but when her mother anxiously inquired whether Nia was "seeing things" again, she replied, "It's nothing. I was thinking!"

They had not understood, of course, and Nia had no intention of trying to explain what she had seen. Her scream had not been a call for help. It had just burst out of her at the sight of something unnatural. She had experienced the same sensation in the churchyard when Gwyn Griffiths had interrupted time, but he'd stolen her breath as well so she had not been able to cry out.

Was it coincidence that her mother was reading about Welsh magicians — magicians who had also been soldiers, kings, and princes? Could Gwyn bring them — even here in safely terraced number six?

She did not doubt that Gwyn was responsible for the mysterious cobweb and for the spider that was now moving so gracefully over carved wooden flowers. Mrs. Lloyd's quiet voice drifted on, soothing herself as well as her children. She seemed almost to be talking to the baby inside her, Nia thought.

The white flower on the windowsill began to glow as the sky behind it deepened into a gloomy twilight. Iolo fell asleep. He couldn't see the spider he had taken from Gwyn Griffiths, hadn't seen the magic he had stolen.

"*Nos da, cariad*," Mrs. Lloyd bent and kissed her daughter.

"Good night, Mom!"

"Better now?"

"Yes, Mom. I'm sorry to be a nuisance."

"You can go back to Tŷ Llŷr again, you know, for a visit. It isn't far."

"No, Mom." Nia smiled and closed her eyes. She had just had a wonderful idea.

Her mother closed the curtains, carefully moving the flower as she did so. "Trust you to find a strange plant," she muttered. "Never seen anything like it."

After school the next day, Nia left Gwyneth Bowen at the school gate, the latter still halfway through a recital of her hamster's vacation misadventures.

"You are rude, Nia Lloyd," Gwyneth called after her. "You don't care about animals, do you? You don't care if Gethin put Sandy in the freezer, do you? You're callous, that's what you are!"

"So's Gethin," Nia shouted back. She had spied Emlyn Llewelyn striding up through the town, always the first to leave school.

Nia tore after him, twisting herself into her backpack and

her jacket. She finally gave up trying to wear them and carried them in a bundle before her.

"Hold on! Emlyn, wait! *Please* wait! *Wait!*" she cried.

Emlyn stopped. He looked back, unsmiling, until Nia caught up with him.

"I've got something for you," she said, "in my backpack. And I want to tell you something about the dress you gave me!"

Emlyn began to stride out again.

Nia had to take little running steps in order to keep up with him. "Hang on! Don't go so fast!" she exclaimed breathlessly.

"Are you coming back with me then?" he asked, slowing his pace a fraction.

"I'll come up to the chapel, but I'd better not come in!" She gulped for air. "I got in trouble yesterday."

"You're always getting in trouble," he remarked, but he slowed down sufficiently for her to heave her backpack onto her shoulders. They were on the bridge now, and the river obliterated all the town sounds.

"Emlyn," she said. "I think I saw your mom last night."

"You what?" He stood quite still, trying to determine her expression, then he shook his head and resumed his frantic pacing.

When he had crossed the bridge, however, he did not continue up the hill to home but leaped down a steep bank where nettles and brambles had been previously attacked to allow a narrow, safe passage to the riverbank.

Nia followed, less skillfully, and found herself, with scratched hands and a dusty skirt, sitting beside Emlyn on the riverbank.

Before them the wide river snaked into the sunlight; behind and all around them, tall reeds concealed their presence from all but a duck, stepping daintily over shining stones.

They sat silently contemplating the water until Emlyn said, "Go on, then!"

"Iolo had a spider in a matchbox." Nia frowned, wondering if she had begun at the wrong place. "The box got wet down by the river and he gave it to me to look after." She plowed on. "It belonged to Gwyn Griffiths. You know about Gwyn Griffiths, don't you?"

"Huh!" was all Emlyn said.

"I mean, I know you know him," Nia floundered. "But he's not like other boys, you know that, don't you? Because of what happened in the churchyard?" She glanced at Emlyn, but he gave her no encouragement.

"Well, this spider, it was like silver and it sort of glowed. I put the box down somewhere in my bedroom and then I . . . well, I hope you don't mind, but I put on your mom's dress. The one your dad gave me yesterday. It was your mom's, wasn't it?"

Emlyn nodded.

"The spider had made this cobweb, like a mirror it was — shining." Nia stared out at the water remembering the glimmering shapes in the web. "And I could see my reflection in it, only it wasn't me, it was your mother, I'm sure it was. She had long dark hair, and big dark eyes, and . . ."

"Don't!" Emlyn jumped up and crashed his way through the dense, dry reeds, then he swung around and came back to her.

He stood looking down at her, with his hands in his pockets and said quietly, "I didn't finish about the night my mom went. I didn't tell you all of it."

"I know," Nia said, and waited.

Emlyn crouched beside her. He spoke quietly and unemotionally. "She was wearing that dress, because it was their wedding anniversary. It was all so good at the beginning: They danced in the field to some music on the old wind-up gramophone. But then it all went wrong." He gritted his teeth, as if biting on a puzzle that still tormented him. "There was this wind that came up from nowhere. It made such a racket, and the baby was crying and crying. It got dark and my mom was going on about the baby, and how we shouldn't be living in a place so small and cold and with no electricity. And my dad got mad — he shouted at her to shut up, and she yelled back and pushed at one of the wooden animals, and somehow it must have knocked the heater over, because the next thing I saw, it was lying on its side and Mom was screaming with flames all around her, but Dad pulled the bedclothes off and wrapped her up in them, and put the fire out!"

"Was she burned?"

Emlyn shrugged. "Not much. Not badly. Dad saved her. But that wasn't the end of it. I went to sleep for a while, and so did Dad, I suppose, because when I woke up I saw him running into the field in his pajamas. I got out of bed and followed him." He took a deep breath, which he exhaled in a long sigh. His next words were spoken to the water, low and stiltingly. "My mom was there, right at the top of the riverbank, where the field goes down and down to the river. She had a big pile of my dad's paintings. She poured paraffin on them, and set them on fire. She was using a long branch to throw them into the river, and little pieces were flying up into the sky. All Dad's work, all burning! And my mom was yelling that she'd go crazy if she stayed here. But we reckoned she was crazy already."

It all made sense now. The warnings. The fear and the suspicion in Pendewi. A fire, and a mother driven crazy. Flames in the air and in the river. "Have you forgiven her?" Nia asked.

"Of course I have." He hugged his knees and almost smiled, remembering perhaps a happier time, when his mother had worn the dress in a sunny place, far away from damp, green Wales. "She's waiting for me, maybe, in that moon she went to, wondering why I haven't come to her. Someone knows where she is, but they're not telling."

Nia took Iolo's matchbox from her bag and opened it a little. "There's something special about this spider," she said. "It belonged to Gwyn, but he's got Fly. You should have this!" She put the box into Emlyn's hand.

He regarded the box. "Can't take a spider for a walk!" he remarked.

"No, but maybe . . . maybe you'll see your mom in a web, like I did."

He didn't reject her suggestion, but he stared at her very hard and put the box in his pocket.

Nia got to her feet. "I'd better go now," she said. "I missed dessert yesterday."

She scrambled up the bank but Emlyn didn't follow, and

when she looked back from the bridge, nothing moved beside the slowly misting river.

There was fruitcake for dessert, everyone's favorite, moist, fruity, and delicious. Two whole loaves were consumed at one sitting.

Nia couldn't sleep afterward. She took her canvas to the bathroom and began to cut a mountain out of mottled gray leather: her mother's gloves, once quite lovely, now torn and marked from holding baskets and babies' hands. Something called her to the window: not a sound, but a feeling somehow, that something was taking place outside that she should see.

The frosted glass distorted form and color in the street. Things changed, but had no features. She slid the window up a fraction and knelt down to peer through the gap. Nothing.

She pulled the window up higher, widening the gap enough to put her head out. Nothing in the street. But up on the bridge something moved, something that was pale yellow in the glare of the streetlights, but was probably white in actuality. Small creatures were crossing the bridge: children, no bigger than herself, for the stones of the bridge wall only came up to their shoulders.

Children out later than midnight! One, two, three, four, five! Nia counted them. Boys or girls? She couldn't tell. They were too far away, their heads concealed in hoods or scarves. Were they the "things" Gwyn had talked about: the icy creatures who had taken his sister? They were on the hill now, walking to where a lamp still burned in the chapel window.

She slid the window down, careless of its rattle, rolled up her canvas, and ran back to bed. She was trembling and clutching Iolo's blue monster, which had fallen from his arms.

Something was all wrong out there. Something terrible had happened. Something unstoppable. Should she run to Emlyn? No, they would stop her, take her. Nia folded herself over the soft woolly monster and closed her eyes tightly. She found herself humming, low and monotonously, her head beneath the blankets, trying to block out what she had seen, telling herself that there were no unearthly children moving toward the chapel.

When she fell asleep at last, it was to dream of herself, almost a baby, playing in the earth near the gate at Tŷ Llŷr. The soil was soft in her hands. She was poking little seeds into the ground, planting and playing. Someone was singing in the lane, and when she looked up she saw a woman with dark hair and a girl beside her, equally dark, holding white flowers, like stars.

The girl knelt beside Nia and laid the flowers on the ground. She took the seeds and planted them in a neat row under the sycamore, where the gate would not disturb them. Her dark hair brushed the earth. She was smiling as she worked, and she smelled of roses.

But you can't dream the smell of roses. Was it a memory?

❋ ❋ ❋

The next morning a dusting of frost outlined the roofs and railings in Pendewi. The frost did not sparkle: There was no sun. Tiny beads of moisture hung in the air, motionless and cold. Damp penetrated the children's clothes: Sleeves clung, shoes slipped. Beside the school gate, violet and yellow irises leaned forlornly, their petals turned to icy paper.

The climate in Pendewi had slipped.

The day had no shape. Within the school a cycle of learning and playing took place, while outside nothing changed. And when the children went home, afternoon seemed like a cold, gray dawn.

Emlyn was not hurrying as he usually did. Nia had to wait for him to fall into step beside her. He seemed to have difficulty in finding his direction, though it only lay forward. He wandered from side to side, jostled by other children, uninterested and dreamy. The street was almost deserted by the time they reached number six.

"Did you . . . did you see anything last night?" Nia ventured, uncertain as to whether Emlyn was even aware of her.

He turned to look at her. The moist air made his face glossy. It looked like a face full of tears. He said nothing.

"The spider?" she gently reminded him. "Did you see a cobweb?"

He seemed to find speech an effort, but at last he said, "Yes!"

"And did you see anything?" She didn't dare mention his mother's name. The climate seemed to forbid it.

He stared at her thoughtfully, then shrugged.

"Tell me, please!"

He shook his head. "No, I can't," he said. He turned away, but Nia tugged at his sleeve.

"Please tell me," she begged. "Did you see your mom?"

He hesitated and then said, "I saw her . . . but I still don't know where she is. There was more in the web. It made me want . . . I can't tell you what I saw!" He shook her off and drew away.

Rejected, Nia swung around and opened the black door, passed through it, and slammed it behind her.

It could have been a stranger out there, not Emlyn who was always full of life and sometimes anger. Was it the children? What had he seen in the web that was tugging at his mind? Would they lead him out of this world to see his mother?

Nia was too distracted to work on her collage that night, and the following day brought her no comfort. Emlyn was more remote than ever. As the days passed, he seemed to fade. He was not eating, she could tell: He had become two sizes thinner than his clothes.

Taking a chance one evening, Nia ran up to the chapel after dinner. "Just going to see Gwyneth," she called to the voices scattered around in number six, and didn't wait for an interrogation.

Mr. Llewelyn was alone, applying giant splotches of yellow to a huge canvas. "Emlyn's not here," he informed Nia. "Been off in the evenings lately. Thought he'd been with you."

"No, he hasn't! I'm worried, Mr. Llewelyn. Emlyn doesn't seem . . . right, if you know what I mean."

"He doesn't, does he?" The painter sighed and scrubbed his brush on the sleeve of his black coveralls.

"What do you think's the matter?" She tried to get his attention by sidling behind his canvas and tapping her foot.

He took up another brush. "I wouldn't know."

"Well, you ought to!" Nia said. "You ought to be worried. I am!"

"Look, girl!" He flung his brush onto a paint-spattered chair beside him. "I am worried. I'm worried about this," he jabbed a finger at his canvas. "It's for an exhibition, see, and it's not ready!"

It hadn't occurred to Nia that adults had exhibitions, too. She shuffled away from him. Mr. Llewelyn was obviously too pre-occupied to notice the change in his son.

She left the chapel and returned to the town slowly, survey-ing hills and woods, watching for a boy who might be walking alone. But Emlyn Llewelyn was hidden with a mysterious some-one or something who was slowly extinguishing him.

CHAPTER TEN
Orchard of the Half Moon

ONLY ONE PERSON COULD HELP. SHE WOULD HAVE TO MAKE A confession, but in secret, somewhere where Gwyn Griffiths would listen and advise.

The cold mist shifted to the mountain. The next morning, Gwyn's black hair glistened in the sun that had appeared to cheer the flowers in Pendewi.

"Is it cold up there on the mountain?" Nia asked, surprising Gwyn and Alun as they talked together in the playground before school.

"It's cold!" Gwyn affirmed.

And I bet you know why, she thought. The boys were being secretive again.

"I found something of yours," she said. "Iolo found it, really. A spider."

Gwyn's reaction was more than she had hoped for. "Where?" he demanded. "Where is it?"

"At home, in a matchbox," she lied. She had to get him to number six somehow, in order to tell him about her problem.

"Come back with us tonight," Alun suggested. "You can pick it up there. Your dad will pick you up afterward, won't he?"

"You've kept it safe?" Gwyn asked.

"Oh, yes!"

Emlyn Llewelyn walked by just then. He looked in their direction. Gwyn returned his cousin's vacant stare: He seemed perturbed by Emlyn's appearance. Something passed between them silently, an understanding that even Alun did not share.

Later, after school, Gwyn went home with the Lloyds.

Mrs. Lloyd was not surprised, but quickly rang Gwyn's mother to ask that he not stay for dinner — she had barely enough sausages for her family.

Gwyn and Alun followed Nia to her room. Iolo was safely munching chips in front of the television.

"Well, where is it, and what has it been doing?"

Gwyn scanned the room, stepping over boxes and toys.

Nia shut the door and leaned against it. She would have to hold Gwyn hostage until she had wrung a promise from him. She did not know whether or not he would help his cousin.

"It's not here," she said flatly.

Gwyn swung around.

"Oh no!" Alun sank on to Nia's bed. "What are you up to, Nia?"

"I gave it to Emlyn Llewelyn!"

Understanding dawned in Gwyn. "Why?" he asked.

"Because it's special. Because it made a cobweb there," she said, pointing at the closet "A shiny cobweb with a woman in it — Emlyn's mother. I was wearing her dress and . . ." Gwyn's expression was beginning to alarm her. "So I gave the spider to Emlyn because you've got Fly and he's got nothing, and . . . and . . ." She clung to the door handle. Words were slipping out of her unevenly and too fast, but she couldn't stop them. "I thought he needed to see his mom but . . . it's all gone wrong! Something's swallowing him up, trying to take him . . . There were children on the bridge after midnight, five of them going to the chapel. They were very pale and —"

"When?" Gwyn's dark eyes seemed to burn.

"Four days ago."

"What? Why didn't you tell me?" Gwyn looked older than any boy she had known. She could feel another presence standing there. It made her limp. "We must go there — stop them — if we're able to!" Gwyn commanded.

"Where?" she cried. "Who?"

"To the chapel!" He didn't answer her second question.

"They won't let her," Alun said. "They've forbidden it."

"We'll see!" Gwyn took Nia by the shoulders and moved her out of his way. He opened the door. "Get the dress!" he commanded, and was gone.

Alun, following his friend, looked back into the room and scolded, "Why can't you do anything right?" He slammed the door behind him.

Muffled voices slipped between the sounds of Catrin's piano and a television announcer: Gwyn's voice and her father's, arguing.

Nia knelt beside her bed. She drew the pale blossomy dress

into the light, then pulled the rolled canvas toward her. She laid it flat. Once she had thought it would be a masterpiece, but it was nothing, just a few scraps of colored stuff, stitched and glued. It would never be finished.

She got to her feet and took her scissors from the drawer, then knelt again. "Nia Can't Do Nothing," she told the poppies that Nain Griffiths had dyed with such care. "Nia is wicked, yes, and stupid. Nia's getting worse. Cut! Cut! Cut! Cutting Miss Oliver's lace, cutting socks! Cut your work, Nia Lloyd! It's back to kindergarten with you! You'll never finish! Never!"

The small, sharp scissors glinted. She began to cut where she had started; where gray smoke drifted from a chimney. Cut! Cut! Cut!

"Don't!" Gwyn Griffiths was there, glaring at her from the door. "Don't!"

Nia was bewildered. She sat back. Her scissors dropped onto the canvas. "How did you know?"

"I know! I'm nosy! I like to know things. Leave it: It's a masterpiece. Roll it up, quick!" Gwyn was a boy again — almost. "Emlyn needs us. Cutting won't help, will it? Will it?" His voice changed with the questions, became that older, wiser voice, full of authority.

"No!" Stunned, Nia rolled up her canvas.

"Hurry!"

"Where are we going?"

"To the chapel."

"Do they know? Mom and Dad?"

"They know. I've fixed it. Come on, and bring the dress!"

Was he all-powerful? Nia pushed her canvas into the secret darkness beneath her bed, picked up the dress, and followed Gwyn.

Down the stairs, across the hall, through the front door, making no effort to tread lightly. The piano shrilled, the television blared, and Mr. and Mrs. Lloyd sat in the kitchen, puzzled. That Gwyn Griffiths! He had a way of making you do things.

Gwyn closed the black door against the Lloyds' mixed bag of noises. "It's OK," he said. "Don't look so downcast. And hurry!" He began to run and Nia pursued him, past Miss Olwen Oliver's gray house, where unlucky lace curtains concealed someone murdering Mendelssohn, past the other chapel where Mary McGoohan was accompanying herself on the organ, past Police Officer Jones, who was humming in the street.

How could Gwyn run up so steep a hill? They were out of the town now, with all the singing sounds behind them. Nia stopped, gasping for air.

"Come on!" Gwyn commanded, and she ran again, clutching the blossom dress, too breathless to wonder what the boy-magician wanted. He was on the chapel steps — she could hear him banging on the blue-and-gold door and then he vanished through it.

Nia reached the chapel, expecting to hear Idris Llewelyn shouting at his nephew. But there were no sounds. She peered inside. Gwyn was standing beside a wooden beast with a fiery orange mane — a unicorn with vacant yellow eyes. "I had forgotten," he said. "I came here once, when we were friends." He seemed to have lost, momentarily, the resolve that had brought him to the place.

"Gwyn, what will we do?" she asked.

"Arianwen's here," he said.

"Arianwen?" Nia saw no one.

"Come in and close the door!"

"But . . ."

"Do it!"

Nia obeyed. She went over to Gwyn who was holding something. She saw the snow spider glowing in the palm of his hand. "I call her Arianwen," he said. "White-silver. She came in the snow, from another world. My sister sent her."

"I don't understand," Nia said.

"But you will believe me, won't you, if I try to tell you?"

"I'll believe!"

He sat on the painter's chair, while she nervously paced around the wooden animals, listening for approaching footsteps, but hearing only Gwyn.

"Nearly two years ago, just after my ninth birthday, I threw an old brooch into the wind. Nain told me to. It was a very ancient brooch, twisted and patterned, silver and bronze. It came from Nain's great-great-grandmother. They say she was a magician. I threw it from the mountain where Bethan disappeared. Snow fell afterward and in the snow on my shoulder I found Arianwen."

Nia gazed at the tiny creature that had lived in her room for a while.

"She came from that other planet," Gwyn went on, "and in her webs she showed me the place where my sister lives now. And I saw the pale children who took her away."

"On the bridge!" Nia cried. "They're here, aren't they?"

Gwyn didn't answer her. "There's something I never told anyone," he said. "Bethan tried to take me back with her and part of me wanted to go, but I belong here. I feel like I've got roots going very deep, down into the time when there were magicians where we live now."

"Emlyn hasn't," Nia said. "Emlyn hasn't got anything. He'll want to go."

"So we must find his mother, and then he'll have something, won't he?"

Nia nodded, knowing that Gwyn was going to ask something of her. "Your auntie Elinor, she isn't out there, is she?"

"No, she's still here, and my dad knows where, but I can't ask him. He thinks he's saved her. He doesn't know Emlyn like we do."

"So, what must I do?"

"Put on the dress!"

"Over my clothes?"

"Over your clothes. Don't be afraid."

"What if someone comes?"

"Do it!" he said solemnly. "Arianwen shows us what she thinks we should see, whether it's hours or years or miles away. Time and distance, they're all the same to her."

Nia slipped the dress over her head. Nothing could interfere with what she and Gwyn were about to do. She felt the cool silky stuff sliding against her skin. If there was a place for spells, then it was surely here. The beasts and butterflies, the long windows, and the many-colored paintings began to drift out of her vision; a boy with brown hair looked down, smiling, from beside a river, and then he was gone behind a shining, widening screen of gossamer. Gwyn's spider was spinning, climbing and falling, weaving and swinging across the wall beside Emlyn's bed.

"Hold tight! Stay very still! Don't run, even if there's pain!" Distance or time had come between her and the voice, but the words, though faint, held her fast. She could see the dress now, in the web that was a mirror. She could see the face that wasn't hers, and the dark hair. She felt unaccountably sad. Beside her a baby cried on and on above the clamor of the wind. She was angry now and shouting, pushing out at the thing that had made her angry.

"What am I doing? Where am I going? Who am I? Gwyn?" She called again, "Gwyn, where are you?"

And the old, wise voice replied, "Stay, Nia! Don't run!"

Flames crept into the web; guttering gold streaks flared into silver, dazzling scarlet fingers caught at the dress and leaped up at her face.

"Help me!" she screamed. "I hate you!" she shouted at someone she couldn't see.

"Don't move, Nia!"

But she couldn't help herself. While small, frightened Nia clung to the space in which she existed, her reflection fled through dark fields carrying a baby. She ran along familiar paths, down into a valley where moonlight made strange shapes and shadows, toward small, ancient trees that bent under a canopy of blossoms — an orchard planted in a crescent — like the moon!

"Where are you going, Nia?"

"I'm going to the moon," she cried. "Of course, the moon! The orchard of the moon! That's where she is — *Perllan yr hanner Lleuad.* Those were her words, but Emlyn only heard her say 'half-moon.' Elinor Llewelyn is in the valley where the cold flowers grow!"

"Come out, Nia! Step back, toward my voice!"

But Nia couldn't move. She was caught in the web. A silly fly bound by strands of the past and another person's life. The spell was too powerful — she couldn't break out.

"Nia! Nia!" The voice was nearer, its power increasing.

Nia held her breath, leaned backward, and took one labored step away from the mirror. As she did so, the glittering glass rippled like the sea and tore apart. Branches of blossoms drifted up through the sky of butterflies, fragmenting into tiny flakes that melted to nothing.

She felt a hand on her shoulder, someone was tapping gently.

When she turned she saw a face as old and as tired as she felt. Gwyn looked utterly exhausted.

"It's as though we've been asleep," she said.

"Not me. I've never worked so hard," he replied. "And we can't rest now. There's more to do."

"Yes," she said meekly.

She stepped out of the dress and laid it on Emlyn's bed while

Gwyn took his spider from the bedpost, where it had come to rest.

"We must go to my aunt now," he said, "and make her come back to her family before it's too late."

Gwyn opened the chapel door and almost walked into Idris Llewelyn who stood there, angry at finding strangers in his home, astonished to see who they were. *"Beth wyt 'in eiseau,* Gwyn Griffiths?" he asked coldly. "What do you want?"

CHAPTER ELEVEN
Soldiers at Dusk

"WE ARE LOOKING FOR YOUR WIFE," GWYN SAID.

"You won't find her here!" Idris Llewelyn took a step toward Gwyn. His fists were clenched.

Gwyn stood his ground. "I know, and it's wrong," he said. "She should be here and she will."

"And who are you, boy, to think that you can reconcile people who were torn apart by your own family?"

Nia saw arrogance flare up in Gwyn, but he resisted the temptation to tell who and what he really was. "I'm going to do what you should have done, long ago, for Emlyn," he said. "You never even bothered to search for your wife, Idris Llewelyn!"

To Nia's horror, the painter laughed. It was not a happy sound. On his face Nia saw a loss that was too unbearable to speak of. She plucked at Gwyn's arm, hoping to stem any more unpleasant truths that he might fling out. But Gwyn had not finished.

"You're going to lose Emlyn, too," he said. "Where is he now?"

Idris Llewelyn wasn't laughing when he answered. "He's

been gone all night!" And turning to Nia, he said, "I'm worried, like you. Find him for me, will you? You're the . . ."

He could not say what he intended, for they were interrupted by the screech of brakes. Gwyn's father glared out from his Land Rover. He could see the children standing inside the open door, beyond Idris Llewelyn. "What're you doing there, Gwyn?" he shouted.

Idris swung around. The two men looked at each other, but said nothing.

Gwyn ran past his uncle, and Nia followed. They climbed into the back of the Land Rover while the engine was still throbbing, but as they drove off, Nia called to the lonely man on the chapel steps, "I'll find him, Mr. Llewelyn. I promise I will!"

Gwyn's father accelerated away from the chapel. The Land Rover roared up the hill. *He committed a crime here*, Nia thought: *kidnapping of a sort, and he doesn't like visiting the scene of his crime.*

Mr. Griffiths was not in a mood for questions it seemed. He drove fast and remained silent. When they reached Tŷ Bryn, however, and the children climbed out, he suddenly asked, "What's Nia Lloyd doing here?"

"She came for dinner," Gwyn replied airily. "We're going up the mountain first to look for something."

Did his father guess? If so, he gave no sign. "What were you doing in that — place?" He couldn't bring himself to say the name.

"They're family," Gwyn retorted. "Everyone needs family!"

He took Nia's hand and led her back onto the lane that

wound and narrowed between thick hedges until it became a sheep track in an open field.

"I'm going to run now," Gwyn warned her. "Can you keep up?"

Nia nodded. His urgency inspired her. "I'll probably race you," she said.

They took off and ran side by side, away from the track and across the steep field where their feet twisted into unaccustomed angles on the hard, sloping land.

Gwyn pulled ahead and reached the valley before her. He waited until she was beside him again, and they looked down into the Orchard of the Half Moon. Frost had snapped at the blossoms, and petals were drifting from the bare branches onto the white flowers beneath.

"They're so bright," Nia said. "You could see them from miles in the air."

"Even farther," muttered Gwyn. "*They* have seen them."

They began to walk down into the valley, through the oak woods and through the flowers that had grown knee high, turning the atmosphere above them into arctic air.

And there was the stone cottage, with a light in the window and smoke curling from the chimney.

Gwyn marched up to the door and knocked. Elinor Llewelyn opened it: She stared at Gwyn for a moment, then smiled, relieved to recognize her visitor. "Gwyn!" she said. "Your father told you!"

"My father told me nothing," Gwyn answered. "Can we come in?"

The woman hesitated. She had not seen Nia at first. "Who is this?" She had become nervous, her hand plucking at a string of beads around her neck.

"It's Nia Lloyd from Tŷ Llŷr. You remember!"

Elinor Llewelyn relaxed. "I thought it might be . . ."

"Bethan?" Gwyn said. "No. She's gone!"

"Of course!" His aunt stood back while they passed her into a dark room that was sparsely furnished. A fire burned in a small black grate. The floorboards were polished, the rug thin and frayed. A boy of two or three played on a bench beside the window.

"This is Geraint," she said, and the boy ran and hid his face in her skirt. "He doesn't see many people," she explained. "Will you sit down? I've got orange juice, I think, and . . . and cookies."

Her voice was ordinary, light, and pleasant, and her face was not as beautiful as the reflection Nia had come to know. This woman looked older, her hair grayer, her eyes deeper and ringed with blue shadows.

"If it wasn't for your father, I wouldn't see a soul," she went on. "I don't go out much. I can't since . . ."

"It must be lonely," Nia said, looking at Emlyn's little brother.

"Well . . . I suppose . . . but . . ." Again the woman seemed unable to form a sentence. She backed away to a tall green cupboard where she found mugs and orange juice, and a package of cookies.

The children took her offerings and sat side by side on the bench among Geraint's toys.

"I think you'll have to come back soon, Auntie Elinor," Gwyn said.

"Come back?" She didn't sit with them but paced nervously beside the fire while little Geraint still clung to her.

"For Emlyn's sake," Gwyn said. "Your other son. He needs to see you. Something is happening to him. They will take him away."

"Take him? But his father is good to him. Ivor, your father, tells me what I need to know. He tells me they're well, my husband and my son. And . . . and I could never go back to them now. . . . I don't like going out."

"Are you ill, Auntie Elinor?" Gwyn asked carefully.

"Ill? Yes!" she replied. "Since the fire, you see. I feel safe here. Your father brings me all I want. And your mom, Glenys, she brings my pills and clothes and toys for Geraint, little things you didn't need, Gwyn."

Nia suddenly remembered the knitted woolen soldier she had found at Tŷ Llŷr.

"Mom said she'd taken them to Oxfam," Gwyn said, almost to himself.

"Oh we do go out, you know," Elinor went on, "early when no one's around, don't we, Geraint? Sometimes we walk to the top of the track. Ivor picks us up in the Land Rover. But we never go to Pendewi. I could never go there again — never. They know what's best for me, don't they?" She began to bite her nails, and Nia was reminded of Alun who used to do that when he was angry and only eight years old. He'd grown out of the habit long ago.

The children stared at Elinor Llewelyn in dismay. She appeared to have an illness that couldn't be named. Could such a frightened and sick person help anyone?

"Who planted those flowers?" Gwyn asked, hoping to jolt his aunt away from memories that distressed her.

"Oh those? A girl." Elinor brightened visibly. "Such a lovely girl, like Bethan, only fair. She stumbled in here one winter, when Geraint was a baby. It was quite wonderful. There'd been a heavy snowfall and we hadn't seen a soul for weeks, but there she was, smiling in at the window. I brought her in, of course, but she didn't seem to feel the cold. Such a funny child; we talked about flowers — I don't know why — and trees, the things that I shared with Bethan." She was calm now, recalling happier times. "Before the girl left," she went on, "she gave me some seeds. 'Plant them under the trees when the snow has melted,' she said, 'and next year you will have flowers in your orchard, flowers like stars, and then we can always find you.'"

Nia felt Gwyn tense beside her. He put his hand on hers, whether to alert her or comfort himself she couldn't tell, but his taut fingers pressed so hard she almost cried out.

"What was her name?" he asked.

"Eirlys!" His aunt was smiling now. "I remember because it's Welsh for snowdrop and she came in the snow."

Gwyn jumped up, pulling Nia with him. "We have to go now," he told his aunt, "and if Emlyn comes here, tell him to wait for us!"

"Emlyn? Oh no! He won't. You mustn't tell him!" The woman instantly became anxious again.

"Don't you want to see him?" Nia asked accusingly.

"I do! I do! I wanted to go back for him so many times. But he knew where I was and he never came. Besides, Idris would have made me stay and I couldn't. You're only children. You don't understand what it's like, wanting something but being afraid. The pills help me to forget, and it's best like that."

Nia began to wish she had never found Elinor Llewelyn. But she had reason to thank her. She pulled the knitted woolen soldier out of her pocket. "Geraint must have dropped this in my garden," she said, "when you went to look after my poppies."

Elinor took the soldier. "So he did!" She smiled. "Thank you, Nia. There was no one there, so I took it upon myself to do a little gardening. It was sad to see lovely Tŷ Llŷr so empty and alone."

Gwyn was already hovering impatiently outside the door. Nia joined him and they began to run, calling good-bye to Elinor Llewelyn, though she had already closed the door.

They ran through the cold flowers and up the path, and this time Nia did not panic, because Gwyn knew the way. He had been there before, when the cottage was deserted, but never since his aunt had lived there. "Dad told me it wasn't safe," Gwyn said. "I didn't think to ask why. I just never bothered to come and look."

When Nia climbed out of the valley, Gwyn had increased the distance between them. He was leaping ahead like a wild animal, but when the farmhouse was in sight he stopped and waited for her.

Nia caught up with him and as they walked down the track

together she asked, "Is your aunt crazy, Gwyn? To run away from her own family, to want to forget them?"

He shook his head. "It was the baby," he said. "Mom told me that mothers do strange things when they are frightened and have a baby. It's protection, like animals and birds. Even our old hens go crazy if you touch their chicks."

"They don't stay crazy," Nia remarked, "when the chicks are grown."

"No. Then it's something I can't explain. My dad went crazy when Bethan disappeared. Perhaps that's why he took special care of Auntie Elinor: He understood. He didn't get better until . . ." Gwyn began to run again.

"Until what?" Nia tried to keep up, though her legs and her ribs were aching.

"Until she came back. Until Eirlys came. I'm scared, Nia," he confessed, "about the flowers she planted."

"She?" Nia was confused.

"Don't you understand? Bethan was Eirlys!"

Nia stood quite still. Pieces of a jigsaw began to move closer. It was like glimpsing a picture through spaces in a cloud. "Bethan?" she breathed.

Gwyn stopped, too. He looked at her. "She must have had seeds with her, in her pocket, when they took her to that other place, and when she came back she brought the seeds with her, only they had changed, like she had. Things that grow in the dark, they're pale. Bethan meant no harm; she only wanted to find her way back to *Perllan yr hanner Lleuad*. But the others will see them. It's like a landmark, shouting at them, and they'll go there, where it's safe and quiet, and they'll wait and take someone — a child — they only take children."

"But they're here already!"

"Only five, you said. There'll be more, many more."

"We must tell someone. Get help."

"You can't explain things like this," Gwyn said. "I know — I've tried. It's too hard for people to understand."

"What can we do?"

"There were three of us once," he muttered. "We're stronger together." He was looking into a space above her head, and then, becoming aware of her scrutiny, he said, "Wait, and think!"

They went into the farmhouse, and Mrs. Griffiths, so happy to see Nia again, did not ask why she was there, but spread the table with hard-boiled eggs and salad and chocolate cake. Nia did her best to do justice to such treats, but her stomach refused to accept more than a few mouthfuls.

"What is it, Dear? Are you coming down with something? How is your family?" Mrs. Griffiths asked, concerned for her favorite visitor.

"Gareth's OK. His leg gets in the way, though," Nia said. "And Mom's tired. Can I take some cake home with me?" She was glad Nerys was not there to glare at her for asking such a question.

"Of course! You might have to wait a while, though. Gwyn's dad wants to fix some fencing on the lane before dark, those Tŷ Llŷr lambs keep getting out."

"Dad never fixed his fences properly," Nia said, and then

because she'd been disloyal, added, "He's good at butchering, though. He's great at that. People come from miles away!"

"That's nice, isn't it?" Mrs. Griffiths smiled uncertainly.

The children helped to clear the table and then went to see Gwyn's white rabbits in the orchard. They were in separate hutches now. Gwyn lifted a hinged door above the female's sleeping quarters and Nia, crouched beside him, saw a bed of soft fur. "It's where the babies will be born," he told her, "but we can't look at them for a while, or she'll eat them. They go a little crazy when they give birth."

"Like your auntie Elinor," Nia said.

"A little like that."

It was much darker than usual for an early summer evening — and cold. The rabbits wouldn't eat their supper of favorite weeds. They sat rigidly on their hind legs, alert and anxious. The birds had fallen silent and even the chorus of ever-hungry lambs had died to an intermittent, plaintive bleat.

Something rippled through the air, not a breeze, but more like a shock wave: a sound like silent screaming.

Gwyn stood up. "Oh no!" he said quietly. "Nia, it's happening." He clutched his thick hair with both hands.

"What?" she asked, frightened by his attitude.

"The children are here, and I didn't call. I didn't make the ship — the seaweed is safe in my drawer. They've come for someone, like they came for Bethan. Can't you feel it?"

Nia didn't need to answer. Cold and dread had caused her to wrap her arms tight around herself.

They stood staring helplessly at each other, and then a

movement by the gate broke the tension and Nain Griffiths came toward them, tall under the apple trees, and dressed in forest green.

"I heard children in the lane," she said, "and I thought it was you."

"We're here," Gwyn said. "We've been here all the time."

"I saw a boy," Nain went on, "and he was alone. But there were others in the woods besides him. I heard them laughing."

"Emlyn knows," Nia whispered. "He knows where his mom is. They're taking him there."

"And the others will be waiting!" Gwyn's voice cracked and then he was seizing Nia's hand, dragging her through the orchard, up the path, and through the gate. "Tell them we've gone to look for someone," he shouted to his grandmother as they pounded toward the field.

Their race, this time, was desperate. Nia felt as though the earth were rocking upside down. They ran on dark rolling clouds in an icy stream of air. The only warmth in the whole world was caught between her hand and Gwyn's, and then he let go of her, and as he drew ahead, she lost him in a mist of freezing vapor.

Her feet and instinct took her to the place, and on the woodland path she caught up with Gwyn as he stood waiting for her. He was watching Emlyn Llewelyn walking toward the Orchard of the Half Moon, and the cottage where his mother was.

Emlyn would soon be with his mom. Nia sighed with relief. She let herself sink onto the path and sat there, relaxed and almost happy. Gwyn walked several paces away from her.

Something about the set of his shoulders, the way he moved, would not let her rest. When she stood again she was petrified by the prospect before her.

There were children crowding into the cottage garden: hundreds of pale, graceful children. They moved in from the trees like streams of thistledown, murmuring softly, their voices gentle as rain.

"They are ancient," Gwyn said. "But only in wisdom. Their bones are not brittle. They will not die — unless they are afraid. I know this!"

Nia knew that Emlyn had forgotten his mother. He could see only the children, so beautiful, almost translucent in the dusk.

"They'll take him, Gwyn," she wanted to cry, but even had she been capable of doing so, Gwyn wouldn't have heard her: He had gone, and something else was where he should have been — a frosty tree stump, a man kneeling under a cloak that reflected all the bright shades in the sky, his hair silver with sunlight.

There were words in the air, rising and falling like insistent, monotonous music. Names perhaps: Math, Lord of Gwynedd, Gwydion, and Gilfaethwy. Names in the air, sung like a sacrament.

And once again, as in the churchyard, time held back and nothing moved, except the flowers, and they were growing. And Nia saw, or maybe dreamed, that from the flowers two men came: soldiers or princes, the way they used to be, with gold at their throats and around their naked arms, with broad, shining swords and patterned shields that gleamed like fire.

They dipped their swords once, twice — as in a rite — together, and where fiery bronze touched the earth, flames came leaping around them.

If nothing else was real, the fire was. Nia could feel the heat on her face. But Emlyn wasn't moving. Either fear or the children seemed to paralyze him, and he would soon be engulfed by flames.

"Help him, Nia!" It was Gwyn's voice. He was beside her, tugging her hand. "He's remembering."

Nia couldn't move.

"I can't do it alone, Nia!"

The fire was white-hot.

"It's an illusion, Nia. It won't hurt you. But I can't keep it!"

"No!" She shrank back.

"We must hold him, or he will go. I am losing myself . . ."

"I can't do nothing," she moaned.

"We're in this together, Nia Lloyd!" the voice hissed in her ear, so close that she felt it in her head. She sprang away from it and ran with one boy, down toward the other who now seemed less substantial than the flames.

But she grasped one hand in both of hers, while Gwyn took the other, and they held and pulled him.

The fire spat and stank. It licked at their feet and clothes like a hungry beast. And Emlyn was rooted in the ground, heavy as oak.

They pulled him until Nia thought that if her body didn't burn it would surely break, and then slowly, he came with them.

Beyond the tall soldiers, Nia could see the children, pressing together, terrified by something that should not exist either in their world or in the place they had invaded. They turned and screamed running through the trees.

A mist of swimming white shapes escaped out onto the mountain and gathered into a cloud of snow: It seemed to shake the earth as it rose into the sky.

Before she fell, Nia thought she saw a billowing sail and a silver prow with dancing creatures on it passing overhead.

CHAPTER TWELVE
A Masterpiece

THEY WERE ALL IN THE KITCHEN AT TŶ BRYN: NIA HARDLY remembered how they had come there.

It had been dark in *Perllan yr hanner Lleuad*, and there had been a wind. They had gone to find Emlyn, she and Gwyn, but the world had rocked and they had fallen, all three of them down together to the place where Emlyn's mother lived.

An earthquake, Gwyn's father called it.

But the bruises on Nia's hands were red, like burns. Her father was there, without his butcher's apron, and he was stroking her head like he used to do, when she was a very little girl.

She couldn't see Gwyn.

Emlyn was there, on the big couch beside his own mother, who held him like she never wanted to let him go, and Geraint was sitting on Idris Llewelyn's knee.

But Nia couldn't see Gwyn.

Gwyn's father was there, grim by the stove. He had known where the children would be when Idris Llewelyn came banging on his door, and summer lightning shattered the sky.

Gwyn wasn't there.

Mrs. Griffiths was pouring tea by the kitchen table. It was she who had carried Nia out of the valley. She had gone with her husband and Idris Llewelyn, under a sky as green as a field of spells. And they had found the children, dazed and bruised, with Elinor Llewelyn crying beside them. The wind had torn her roof away.

"Where is Gwyn?" Nia cried.

They all looked at her and Gwyn's mother said gently, "He's resting, Dear."

"Let me see him!"

"He's asleep!"

She didn't believe them. "I want to see him!" she demanded.

So Mrs. Griffiths took Nia into the front room and she saw Gwyn lying in a big armchair with a blanket over him. His eyes were closed and his face, beneath the cloud of black hair, looked like paper.

"The doctor's coming soon," Mrs. Griffiths told her. "He'll help Gwyn get back to his old self."

It seemed then that, not only Nia's voice, but her whole body yelled, "He's not asleep!" And tears spilled out in a wave that left her breathless. She wiped them away again and again, as though they had no business there, when there were so many things to consider.

Mr. Griffiths gripped her shoulders. "He's not gone, girl," he said. "He'll be OK. Come away now."

As he drew her into the hallway, the front door opened and Nain Griffiths stood there in a cloak that shone darkly like crow feathers.

"Give me my boy!" she said.

Without a word, Mr. Griffiths went and lifted his son out of the chair. He put Gwyn, wrapped in the blanket, into Nain's arms, and although he was ten years old, his grandmother carried him into the night, as if he was nothing but a shadow.

❄ ❄ ❄

Summer came swiftly after the storm: a scorching summer of cloudless skies and hours of sunshine that stretched from early dawn till long after bedtime.

Morgan the Smithy and his three sons worked shirtless outside. Nia watched them in the evenings, splashing themselves cool in the river, singing and swearing cheerfully at one another.

Six weeks went by, and in those weeks so many things happened it was as if a train had thundered through the valley, throwing out goodwill like birthday presents.

Idris Llewelyn sold his yellow-patterned painting to a gallery in London and they wanted more if he could do them. They took his photo for the newspapers, with his wife and his two sons. How proud he was in his black coveralls, holding a check for a thousand pounds.

Emlyn came back to school, quite his old self again, only now he was "that Emlyn whose dad sells paintings," and children lined up to talk to him.

Elinor Llewelyn left the cottage in the Orchard of the Half Moon — she couldn't stay after her roof had fallen in. She and Geraint went to live in the Griffithses' farmhouse. She saw Emlyn and her husband every day, but nothing would persuade her to move back to the chapel. This unsatisfactory situation might have continued, had help not arrived from quite an unexpected quarter.

One afternoon Mr. Lloyd came out of his shop, hot and a little irritable. It wasn't easy trying to sell meat from the window and keep it cool. His impatient family waited for their tea while he scrupulously scrubbed his hands in the sink, and then he said, in an offhand way, "Would Idris Llewelyn like to live in Tŷ Llŷr? His wife would go there, I'm sure. There'd be no money involved — well not much — no one else wants it, and it'll fall down if it's empty any longer. He can keep his chapel, just for work."

Nia ran and hugged him, bloody apron and all.

"Hold on, girl," he laughed. "They haven't agreed. And we'll need to work on fixing the house up."

Of course, they did agree. Elinor had always loved Tŷ Llŷr, and Idris could turn any sort of building into a home.

He and Ivor Griffiths, reconciled at last, spent a night in the Red Dragon Inn, with Iestyn Lloyd, to seal the buying of Tŷ Llŷr. It was a night the town never forgot. They called it Llewelyn's Night, for he was like a returning prince, now that he had a house and a wife, two fine sons, and money in the bank. The Pendewi Male Choir was there, and you could hear the singing all the way to the sea.

But Nia remembered it because it was the night she finished her picture. She took the tiny pieces she had cut from the hem of Elinor Llewelyn's dress and sewed them in a half circle on the side of the mountain, and beneath them she glued clusters of silver glitter, so that they appeared to reflect the stars in her midnight sky.

It was finished — yet incomplete.

She could have asked Emlyn's advice: He was an acceptable visitor now, and she could have taken it to Idris Llewelyn in his chapel studio, to ask what was missing. But she waited until Gwyn Griffiths had recovered.

He came to visit them a week after Llewelyn's Night. He was still pale, but his grandmother's herbs had brought him to life. If it was shock that he had suffered from, as his father said it was, then why did his eyes look so weary and why did he stumble on the stairs? Nia knew that it was exhaustion, that he'd put too much of himself into the spell that had brought ghosts back to Wales, to save his cousin.

After tea, when the other boys were playing in the river, Nia took Gwyn indoors to see her work.

She laid it out on the floor of her room and sat back, watching him.

Gwyn knelt beside the canvas. He observed it solemnly, while Nia waited anxiously.

"It's beautiful, Nia!" he said at last. "It's a masterpiece. It's magic. . . ."

"But," she said anxiously, "something's missing, isn't it?"

Gwyn frowned. "No. Not really, it's only . . . There's no one there — no people. Only birds and sheep."

"Oh!" She gazed at the canvas for a moment. "People change," she said. "They go and they die!"

Gwyn looked at her. "In a way," he said. Then he left her and went to join Alun by the river.

When he left, she cut the shape of a girl out of her mother's shell-gray tights, and put it where the starry flowers grew in *Perllan yr hanner Lleuad*. And in the oak woods she put a starling's feather: It could have been a holly tree or a shining cloak. Beyond the feather, she glued strips of brown silk sprinkled with gold glitter, and in the center of each strip, a silver circle, like the shield of a soldier, a prince — or a magician!

Her landscape was complete.

The following day the children in grade three had to submit their project work.

They were all in the assembly hall, along with Miss Powell and the older children from grade four as well, who were brought in to help Mr. James with his judging. The long table at the end of the hall was filling with papers, books, and models. Gwyneth Bowen's story was three workbooks long, and her illustrations drew sighs of envy and admiration.

Then it was Nia's turn. She handed Mr. James her long roll of canvas and he looked at her apprehensively before unrolling it. For a second, Nia panicked. It was upside down. They wouldn't understand. Then Miss Powell caught the other end and they held it up, all six feet of it, high enough for everyone to see.

It went dead quiet and Nia's nose began to itch, though it hadn't done so for nearly a month, and she felt Gwyneth Bowen glaring at her.

There was sunlight in the hall. The stars, streams, and flowers glittered. Nia had never seen her picture from a distance. She could hardly believe it was she who had put those brilliant colors and shapes together.

"Nia Lloyd, did anyone help you with this?" Mr. James asked, astonished and disbelieving.

"No sir!" Nia tried to say, but her throat had gone dry and the words came out as a guilty sort of cough.

Then, from the back of the room, Emlyn Llewelyn shouted, "Nia did it herself, sir. I know. You can ask my dad. And don't you ever say she didn't!"

Everyone looked at him and then at Nia who felt very hot, and Mr. James was too taken aback to make an issue of the impudence. "Well!" he said, and, "By golly, this is a . . ."

He didn't realize he was stuttering until everyone began to laugh, and he felt Miss Powell staring at him.

"I think this is it, children, don't you?" he said, remembering his dignity. "A masterpiece! We'll hang it right in the middle! Pride of place! *Llongyfarchiadau*, Nia Lloyd! Congratulations! By golly, this is something for the papers!"

Then everyone was clapping and stamping and shouting, "Hooray!" and slapping Nia on the back. And when she left the assembly hall she knew she would never be "Nia Can't Do Nothing" again.

She went up to Llewelyn's chapel that evening. It was the last night that it would be a home and although the painter would come to work there, it would never be quite the same again.

The Griffiths family was there. The boys were kicking a ball around the field, little Geraint following Emlyn and screaming with delight. The parents watched and murmured to one another.

Nia stepped up onto the railing and looked over. She couldn't go in. They were all together now, one family, but not hers. She clung to the railing and watched them for a long time. They never saw her. She had brought them together, just as she'd always intended.

She stepped down into the road and became aware that someone was shouting her name.

Alun was running up the hill. "It's come, Nia! The baby! Mom wants you!" he called.

Nia flew down toward him but Emlyn must have seen her. He came out onto the road and shouted, "Nia! You'll come to Tŷ Llŷr, won't you? There's going to be loads of plums, and the flowers are yours, they always will be!"

But she was too breathless to reply or turn to him. There were so many thoughts racing through her mind, above all the sudden realization that she wasn't in the middle anymore.

If she was a little apprehensive ascending the last flight of stairs, she forgot everything when she found her family, crushed into the few spaces around the huge bed.

The boys were sitting on it, her sisters leaning on one side with Mr. Lloyd on the other.

Mrs. Bennett, the midwife, was in the only chair. The baby had come so quickly that she was still breathless from bicycling two miles and running up three flights of stairs.

"Come and see your sister, Nia," Mrs. Lloyd said. "She's beautiful! And so like you!"

"Give her a name, girl!" Mr. Lloyd drew her closer to the bed, where the baby lay in her mother's arms.

"It's your turn, Nia, to name the baby!" Catrin reminded her.

Nia approached, self-conscious and diffident. The baby looked solemnly out of her knitted white cocoon: Her eyes were round and dark as berries. There was only one name for a baby like that.

"Let's call her Bethan!" Nia said.

Read the first chapter of

THE CHESTNUT SOLDIER

THE MAGICIAN TRILOGY

BOOK THREE

Coming April 2007

CHAPTER ONE

THE PRINCE DID NOT COME ENTIRELY UNANNOUNCED. THERE were messages. They slipped through the air and kindled Gwyn's fingers; the joints ached, things fell out of his grasp, and he knew something was on its way.

They had nearly finished the barn; it needed only a few extra nails on the roof to secure it from the wild winds that were bound to come, and planks to fit for the lambing pens. That was Gwyn's task. He had never been much of a carpenter and today he was proving to be a disaster. But he could not pretend that cold or damp was causing his clumsiness. A huge September sun glared across the mountains, burning the breeze. The air was stifling!

Gwyn hated hammering on such a day. Sounds seemed to sweep, unimpeded, into every secret place, and with his father on the roof banging away at corrugated iron, the clamor was deafening.

"Aww!" Gwyn dropped his hammer on to a bucket of nails and thrust his fist against his mouth.

"What've you done, boy?" Ivor Griffiths called from his perch.

"Hammered my thumb!"

"You need glasses!"

"Take after you then, don't I?" It was a family joke, Ivor's glasses. They were always streaked with mud, or lost. Gwyn could see them now, balanced on a pile of planks.

"Is it bad?" his father asked.

"Mmm!" Pain began to get the better of Gwyn; the numbing ache aggravated by a bruised and bleeding thumbnail.

"Better go and see Mom," his father suggested. "You're no good wounded, are you?"

"No, Dad!" Gwyn slid a chisel into his pocket, wondering why he felt compelled to do this. Perhaps something at home needed his attention. He didn't know, then, what it would be.

He stuck his thumb in his mouth and jogged down the mountain track toward the farmhouse. In spite of the urgency he could not resist a look back at the barn. It would be a grand shelter for the ewes, something to be proud of, for they'd done it all themselves: he and his dad, his cousin Emlyn, and Uncle Idris. It was a family affair.

"Idiot!" Gwyn told himself. "There's nothing here." It was such a bright and beautiful day. He could see it all from his high field and all was well. Nothing threatened from the valley, where trees glowed with early autumn color. There were no phantoms hiding in the mountains that stretched calm and splendid under an empty sky. But the warning in his hands could not be ignored.

He was tired of magic, of intuition, and the unnatural power that rippled through him sometimes. Once, he'd been tall for his age. But in four years he'd hardly grown. Now information slipped in and out of his mind too swiftly for him to make sense of it. In class he dreamed, wondered about the distance between stars instead of trees, drew crescents where he should have made straight lines, forgot his English, and wrote Welsh poetry that no one understood.

Perhaps soon, he thought, *when I am thirteen, the wizard in me will fade away and I will grow and be like an average boy.* To be average was Gwyn's greatest wish.

Bending his head over his injured thumb, Gwyn began to run, really hard this time, so that the stitch in his side would distract him from the painful little hints of bad tidings.

His mother was in the kitchen, baking for the school fair. Her face glowed pink, with triumph or the unnatural temperature, Gwyn couldn't guess which. The long table was mounded with extravagantly decorated cakes and the stove was still roaring. Mrs. Griffiths had a reputation to maintain. Her cooking won prizes. Two sticky flypapers hung above the table, diverting insects from chocolate sponges, iced buns, jammy gâteaux, and waves of bara brith. The papers buzzed with dead and dying creatures.

"Oh! It's hot in here, Mom!" Gwyn exclaimed. "How can you stand it?"

"I've got to, haven't I?" Mrs Griffiths mopped her flushed cheeks with a damp tissue. "Your dad's not moved the muck from the yard and if I open the window there'll be stench and bluebottles all through the house. I don't know how the wasps get in, the sly things!"

"Dad's still on the barn. He's nearly done. It's going to be just grand, Mom!"

"I know! I know! What've you done then?" she eyed Gwyn's bloody thumb.

"Hammered my nail, didn't I?" Gwyn grinned sheepishly.

"You're not going to tell me it was the cold that made you clumsy?"

"Naw! It was the sun, made my eyes water." It was a pretty lame excuse since he'd been inside the barn, but it would have to do. He gave up all attempt at bravery and grimaced. "It hurts, Mom!"

"Come on then, let's put it under the cold tap!" His mother took his hand.

The water was icy. It calmed the pain in his thumb but now his fingers tingled unbearably. Something needed to be done, but what? "That's enough! I'm OK!" He pulled his hand away.

"It's still bleeding, Gwyn. I'll have to bandage it." His mother brought a first-aid box from the cupboard by the sink. "Tch! I've no wide bandages. Hold still!"

Gwyn hopped from foot to foot. Things took so long when you needed to be finished with them.

"What's your hurry, boy?" His mother spread yellow cream onto the torn nail and began to wrap it up. "Anyone would think there was a time bomb here!"

Perhaps there is, of a sort, Gwyn thought.

The bandage swelled into a giant grub.

His father peered in through the window. He tapped a pane. "I'm off to Pendewi, Gwyn. Want to come?"

"I . . . well . . ." Was it here, or was it there that he was needed?

"Make up your mind, boy. I'm late as it is!" Mr. Griffiths vanished.

"Go on, Gwyn. Go and have a chat with Alun." His mother pushed him gently away.

The Land Rover hustled noisily from the lane.

Gwyn hovered by the door. "OK," he said and rushed through it. He needed to talk to someone.

As he flung himself into the seat beside his father, he realized it was not Alun he wanted to see, but Nia, Alun's sister.

Alun was a good friend and would be, probably forever, but he drew away from magic and all talk of it. Only Nia understood. Only she had glimpsed events beyond the world that surrounded her, and welcomed spells as naturally as she did spring flowers.

The journey to Pendewi took twenty minutes. It would have taken ten if the lane had not been so steep. The town was only five miles away. But the Griffiths' farm was the highest on the mountain. It lay at the end of a track that was hardly more than a twisting channel carved into the rock. Even in the Land Rover, progress was slow until they reached the main road. Then it was a few minutes of racing with coast-bound cars and trailers, over a bridge and down into the town.

Traffic between the Lloyds' and the Griffithses' was frequent.

They had been neighbors until the mountain drove the Lloyds down to the valley. Its pitiless winters had been too much for Iestyn Lloyd, father of eight. Such a man must be master of his home so he had left farming and sold his old house to Gwyn's uncle Idris. Now Iestyn was a butcher in Pendewi and doing very nicely. But five miles and a different way of life could not interrupt a friendship which was as constant as time.

The Lloyds lived at number six High Street. Their tall terraced house had two doors, one blue for the shop, the other black for the family. Gwyn and his father went into the shop. Iestyn was placing chickens onto shiny trays in the window. "Alun's not here," he told Gwyn. "Gone swimming with the twins."

"Doesn't matter," Gwyn said.

"Wife's out, too, showing the baby off again!" Iestyn gave a smug wink.

"I'll go and see Nia!"

Leaving the men to discuss the price of lamb, Gwyn turned through a door that led into the house beyond; the Lloyds' living quarters.

It was a rare, quiet moment in a house that held eight children.

Gwyn walked down the passage to the open back door, but he did not step into what they called the garden, a small square of dry grass confined by ivy-covered walls and the back of the house. In one wall a glass pane revealed scarlet carcasses hanging in the butcher's room. And beside the low wall that held the garden back from the river, Nia had planted bright flowers, almost, it seemed, as a distraction from the lifeless gaudy things behind her father's window.

Today, however, the distraction came from elsewhere. The boys had made a hammock and slung it between the branches of next-door's apple tree. They had joined rope and twine and their mother's rags into a bright lattice, and where the rags were knotted, thin strips of color floated like tiny breeze-blown flags.

Catrin was lying in the hammock while Iolo, who was eight, gently set the swing in motion.

Catrin was sixteen; she had cornflower blue eyes and abundant yellow hair. Gwyn thought she was probably the most beautiful girl in Wales. Lately he had found it difficult to talk to her. He did not even come up to her shoulder.

Catrin turned and waved. She looked like a princess, swinging in a basket of silk ribbons.

"I'm looking for Nia," Gwyn mumbled and stepped back into the passage. He could hear voices at the top of the house, Nerys and Nia arguing.

He walked to the bottom of the stairs but decided against interrupting.

The shouting subsided. A door slammed.

Gwyn sank onto the only seat in the hall; a low oak box where outgrown boots and shoes waited for the next child to find and approve them.

The hall was cool and shady. Gwyn expected to be soothed, but if anything his agitation increased.

Could it be here, the menace that was troubling his hands?

Surely nothing could invade this cozy house. It was too crammed with children; it was barricaded with noise, constant movement, and the smell of washing. Could a demon slip through a swinging door or slide on a draft beneath loose windows? And if so, where could it hide? None of the small, low-beamed rooms was empty for long.

Gwyn hummed tunelessly.

And then, from the top of a bookcase the telephone shrilled. He stared at the instrument, vibrating on its perch, hoping that someone would come to put it out of its misery. Perhaps he should answer it? Take a message. But he found that he couldn't touch it. He was about to escape through the front door when Iolo bounded in exclaiming, "Is it for me? I bet it is! My friend said he'd call."

Perhaps Iolo was too eager, for the receiver slipped out of his hand and swung on its black cord, back and forth across the dusty books. For some reason Iolo couldn't touch it either. He shrank from it as a voice called from the instrument, "Who is there? Who is there?" And Nia ran down the stairs.

Taking in the scene she stepped toward the telephone ready for conversation but suddenly she recoiled. And still the receiver swung on its shiny cord, impelled by nothing, unless it was the voice tumbling through it.

All three watched it helplessly, until it came to rest and then words spilled toward the reluctant children, clear and strong: a man's voice deep and anxious, "Who is there? Who is there?"

It was only a voice but, somehow, as potent as electricity, and Gwyn was reminded of a black snake he'd heard of, very small and unremarkable, but with enough venom in its fangs to kill an army.

He clasped his hands and leaned over them as little stabs of pain shot through his fingers right up to his elbows.

"What've you done to your thumb?" Nia inquired, glad to find a reason for ignoring the voice.

"Been clumsy again," he said.

Catrin came into the hall. "What's the matter with you three?" she asked. "There's someone on the phone," and without waiting for them to reply she took the receiver and said, "Catrin Lloyd here! Who is it you want?" Her hair was all tangled gold from the swing.

"Catrin?" Gwyn could hear the voice. "Ah, Catrin," and it seemed to sigh. "It's Evan here. Your cousin, Evan Llyr!"

"Evan Llyr!" Catrin repeated the name, frowning.

"You remember me?"

"I . . . I remember . . ."

"I don't believe you do." Here, a deep laugh. "It's been ten years, you were a little child."

"I was six."

"How many of you are there now?"

"Eight."

"Eight?" There was an exclamation and a sentence inaudible to the listeners, except the words, ". . . and you're the eldest?"

"No, there's Nerys."

The voice softened, its words maddeningly muffled.

"You're coming here?" Catrin said.

Gwyn didn't like the way she pulled at her tangled curls, as though the voice was watching her.

"No, Mom's not at home . . . I'll tell her . . . Evan Llyr is on his way . . . Oh, you'll be welcome, sure . . ." Catrin's free hand was at her throat, the other gripped the receiver.

They were only words, ordinary, pleasant words spoken far away but they slid through the air like a spell.

Gwyn wanted to shout, "Leave it! Run, before he catches you!"

"Good-bye, now!" Catrin replaced the receiver. Her cheeks were pink. It could have been the heat. "You're a funny bunch, you are," she said. "Why didn't you answer the poor man?"

"It wasn't for us," Nia said, illogically.

"You can take messages, can't you?"

Nia chewed her lip but was not put down. "Not that sort," she muttered.

"Sometimes you're very silly!" Catrin swung away and ran up the stairs. Her feet were bare and her swirling skirt made mysterious shadows on her long golden legs.

Gwyn, watching Catrin, knew that Nia was watching him. He had never heard the sisters quarrel. Nia had come off badly. Nerys could scold, and did, often. Catrin was always kind.

Remembering the scene, weeks later, Gwyn wondered if that was when the strife began.

Iolo ran back outside, leaving Gwyn and Nia alone. Nia was troubled and Gwyn didn't know how to comfort her. He had wanted to see her but the disembodied voice had confused him and he couldn't remember his purpose.

"I wish I could grow," he suddenly confided.

"Grow?" Nia said, as though the word had no meaning.

"You can't say you haven't noticed. Alun's much taller than me now."

"Alun's taller than everyone."

"Sometimes I think I'll never grow again," Gwyn rambled on, almost to himself. "I'll be a dwarfish sort of man, thoughts rattling in my brain beside the magic and never getting clear of it."

"You'll grow," Nia said. It sounded automatic. She was still not herself.

"You coming, boy?" His father emerged through a door from the butcher's shop. He was carrying a joint of meat, several red-stained bags, and the Lloyds' evening paper.

"Yes, Dad!" Gwyn levered himself up from the chest. The tingling in his hands had eased. All at once he realized it was he who had, somehow, prevented Nia and Iolo from touching the telephone, and he didn't know why. But whoever he is, this Evan Llyr, Gwyn thought, he has already reached Catrin and I can't fix that.

He followed his father to the front door but before leaving he turned to Nia and asked, "Are you all right?" He spoke softly, not wishing to call attention to his concern for the girl.

Nia nodded and replied, "Mind your fingers."

He knew she was not referring to his injured thumb. She understood. Nia, too, experienced irrational stabs of fear.

At least they had each other.

Something had invaded the house. They didn't know what it was, but it still smoldered there.

❄ ❄ ❄

Mr. Griffiths did not drive straight home. He pulled up where the mountain lane began to twist through arches of yellowing ash trees. The Land Rover lurched onto a bank that had become part of the crumbling wall it supported. Beyond the wall a cottage could be glimpsed, through a jungle of giant shrubs and plants.

"I've got Nain's bacon here," Mr. Griffiths said. "Coming in to see her?"

"No," Gwyn replied.

"What's wrong, boy? Why d'you keep avoiding your grandmother? What's the trouble between you?"

"No trouble, Dad." Gwyn drew himself into the back of the seat. "I don't want to go in."

"Don't hurt her! It's not much to ask, a quick visit, only take five minutes." Mr. Griffiths opened the door and looked hopefully at his son. "You were once so close, Gwyn, but you haven't visited her for weeks."

"No need to tell her I'm here," Gwyn said.

His father left him in peace. Gwyn watched him gradually disappear into the ocean of plants. You couldn't see the front door anymore.

Ashamed and angry with himself, Gwyn huddled down into his seat. His grandmother had a peephole through the plants, he knew, because once he'd been on the other side of her narrow window and seen his father herding his black cows up the lane.

He couldn't go in there anymore. Nain asked too much of him. Four years ago, on his ninth birthday, his grandmother had given him five gifts that had changed his life. For with the gifts had come the knowledge that he was a descendant of Gwydion, the magician, and inheritor of his power. Gwydion, who sent messages like fire in his fingers, who drew a force from him that could even search the stars.

Once Gwyn had been so triumphant, so proud of his talent; but being different led to loneliness. He had to watch himself, to curb his anger for fear of hurting. Being extraordinary was not a happy state.

But wrapped in her dark herbal-scented house, Nain always wanted more from him. Her own great-great-grandmother had been a witch, but she herself hadn't the power, so she wanted his, even when there was nothing to be done. She couldn't see that it was stunting him — Nain was as tall as her own front door.

One of those birthday gifts was a small carving of a mutilated horse that Gwyn must never use, nor leave where it might tempt a stranger to set it free, for it held the spirit of a demon prince. Gwyn's fingers burned again and he exclaimed aloud in surprise, wondering why he remembered the Lloyds' telephone when he thought of the broken horse, and why he heard the disembodied voice crying, "Who is there?"

Mr. Griffiths appeared at the gate. He looked grim. When he had climbed in beside Gwyn he said, "She knew you were here. It's cruel not to see her."

"I'm sorry!" He could not explain the reason to his father. Gwyn remained in his mute huddle.

His silence infuriated his father. "I won't force you, Gwyn, you know that," Mr. Griffiths spoke quietly at first and then he suddenly railed, "but, by God, you're a mean-spirited little beast."

And you're a terror for losing your temper, Gwyn thought, but he said nothing.

Mr. Griffiths wrenched the hand brake free and jabbed at the ignition. The Land Rover rocked off the bank and roared up the lane, its occupants divided by an unwelcome quarrel.

The kitchen table was laid for tea when they reached home. Cans, bowls, and messy ingredients had vanished.

"A genius you are, Glenys," Ivor Griffiths told his wife.

Rows of cakes in plastic packaging were stacked on the dresser, neat as soldiers on parade.

"Wow!" breathed Gwyn. "You'll break a record with all this."

His mother beamed and poured the tea so Gwyn couldn't be unkind and run upstairs just then. He knew now why he'd slipped a chisel into his pocket.

His father relaxed after his meal. He sat in his big armchair and read Iestyn Lloyd's newspaper.

Gwyn went up to his room. He stared at the rug beside his bed for a full minute, then he rolled it up, revealing five dusty floorboards. The center board had been replaced long ago by three short planks, one only half a yard long. The nails securing this board were obvious and shiny; they were only four years old. The others, scattered across the floor, brown and invisible, were more than two hundred.

Gwyn eased his chisel into a narrow gap at one end of the short board, and began to lever it up, wondering, as he worked, why he was invading the hiding place. Was it only for reassurance? The thing that he'd imprisoned there four years ago could surely not have escaped.

It was easier than he had imagined. Two nails suddenly snapped free, then the others. The board was loose. Gently, Gwyn lifted it away.

Dust covered the hidden object in a thin gray film but did not conceal it. He experienced a tiny jolt of fear, but forced himself to bring into the light a small, four-legged, wooden creature.

He blew the dust away and it drifted into the warm air, some settling on his hands. It was smaller than he remembered and even more hideous, a mockery of a horse, with severed ears and tail, blank lidless eyes, and teeth bared forever in what could only be despair.

And Gwyn felt pity as he had four years before and a longing to do what he must never do — set the captured demon free and take away its pain. But the injunction still remained on a scrap of dappled paper tied to the creature's neck, *"Dim hon!* Not this!" scrawled in a witch's hand.

If he'd been rational then, he'd have replaced the horse in

that safest of hiding places, but panic and his aching fingers distracted him, caused him to hover about the room, rumbling in drawers and cupboards. At length he chose a beam set high into the back wall but protruding ten inches from it: a narrow shelf where he kept his most precious possessions.

He climbed onto the bed and pushed the horse between a lump of glittering quartz and a crowd of pearly shells. The other gifts were there too, the yellow scarf, folded tight; a dry stick of seaweed; and the pipe that his ancestors had flung to Gwyn through time so that he might hear voices inaudible to other mortals. Once, he'd heard a sound he wished he could forget.

The last gift was resting in a tiny circle of gossamer at the end of the beam: Arianwen, the spider, sent by his lost sister from another world, in exchange for an ancient metal brooch.

"What d'you think, Arianwen?" Gwyn spread his fingers invitingly along the beam. "Will I grow? Is the magic shrinking me? I'm tired of it, see. It hurts. I don't want it anymore!"

The spider crept toward him and, as she moved into deep shadow beneath the beam, a cloud of glowing particles spiraled round her.

Gwyn took her into his hand. "There," he said. "I didn't mean it!" She was part of the magic and he would never reject her. He could hardly feel her, but the coolness of her silvery body soothed his tingling fingers.

Gently, he dropped her onto the broken horse. "Guard it for a while," he said. "I don't know what to do."

But the little spider ran away from the dark creature and Gwyn couldn't blame her. Something writhed in there, someone glared out from the dead eyes: a mad, imprisoned prince. But what had it to do with that lost voice clutching at Catrin through a telephone receiver?

Gwyn stepped away and jumped off his bed. "I'm not sleeping with you there," he told the horse. "I'll move you later." He left the room, closing the door tight.

Behind the horse's terrible injuries, someone smiled to himself. He had waited for two thousand years; what did a few days matter? The man he had summoned was drawing closer.